PE

BERGERAC AN[...]

Andrew Saville is the pseudonym of an award-winning crime writer who lives in Gloucestershire.

Other titles in this series:

Already published

ANDREW SAVILLE

BERGERAC
AND THE
FATAL
WEAKNESS

PENGUIN BOOKS

PENGUIN BOOKS

Published by the Penguin Group

27 Wrights Lane, London w8 5tz, England

Viking Penguin Inc., 40 West 23rd Street, New York, New York 10010, USA

Penguin Books Australia Ltd, Ringwood, Victoria, Australia

Penguin Books Canada Ltd, 2801 John Street, Markham, Ontario, Canada l3r 1b4

Penguin Books (NZ) Ltd, 182–190 Wairau Road, Auckland 10, New Zealand

Penguin Books Ltd, Registered Offices: Harmondsworth, Middlesex, England

Published in Penguin Books 1988

Filmset in 10/12 Linotron Baskerville

by Centracet

Made and printed in Great Britain by

Richard Clay Ltd, Bungay, Suffolk

CHAPTER
I

The man in the cell was dreaming.

Even as he slept, he knew it was the old dream. His limbs were heavy with sleep and alcohol. The room should have been as familiar as his own name, yet it might have belonged to a stranger. It looked smaller than usual, perhaps because of the visitors. It was unfamiliar in other ways too – the carpet rippled like water in a breeze and one of the plastic-covered armchairs was lying on its back.

Yes, he was drunk again. And now, of all times –

Still in the dream, he tried to focus his eyes. He had to get up; he had to do something – something more important than he had ever had to do before. He had to save his wife.

She was on the floor. He knew that, though he couldn't see her. He could see the back of the man crouching beside her, his body masking hers. The other visitor, a big woman, must be standing near her head. The woman held a long knife with a serrated blade.

The man said something. The words were indistinct, but the intonation sounded like a question.

The woman shook her head. 'No point, Ronny.' Her eyes flicked towards the dreamer. 'He's dead to the world. Stoned out of his tiny mind.'

'He's drunk as a lord, Jim.'

The uniformed sergeant led the way down the echoing corridor. The bunch of keys jangled in his hand.

'What makes you think he's one of ours?' Bergerac asked.

'Stands to reason.' Sergeant Corrance glanced over his shoulder. 'For a start, he looks like a dago. And he had a dry-cleaning ticket on him – in the name of Alvaro Ferreira.' Corrance sniffed. 'Can't get much more foreign than that.'

Bergerac sighed. Corrance was on the verge of retirement and he had a well-deserved reputation as the laziest man in the Jersey States Police. If any other sergeant had been on this shift, he would have handled the case himself, not passed it on to the Bureau. It was a routine drunk-and-disorderly, by the sound of it, nothing more.

But not Corrance. The old sergeant had built his career on the principle that his first duty was to pass the buck. The man in the cells had a foreign name – so therefore he came within the jurisdiction of the Bureau des Etrangers; he was nothing to do with Corrance.

Corrance stopped in front of a door and fumbled with the bunch of keys. Now the buck was safely out of his hands he was prepared to be helpful.

'They picked him up in Royal Square about 3 a.m. He was chucking empty beer cans at the statue. Didn't actually hit it, they said, but it's the thought that counts.'

Breathing heavily, Corrance peered through the judas window.

'Still sleeping,' he said. 'Where does he think he is? The Ritz?'

He inserted a key into the lock.

'When they picked him up,' Corrance went on, 'he tried to scarper. How stupid can you get? By all accounts he could barely walk, let alone run. They put him in the car and he blacked out.' Corrance's fat, white face split into a smile. 'Know what Jeff said?'

Bergerac looked surreptitiously at his watch and smothered a yawn. 'Jeff?'

'Constable Yardley – he was driving. He said the dago blacked out because he was terrified. Can you beat it?'

Bergerac shrugged and said nothing. It wasn't such a ridiculous idea. Alvaro Ferreira sounded Portuguese; the man was probably one of the immigrants who found work in one of Jersey's service industries. Many immigrant workers came to Jersey with a justifiable fear of authority, especially when authority wore a uniform.

Corrance opened the door. Ferreira lay face downwards on the little bed. The blankets had slipped off him. He wore black trousers and a grubby white shirt. He twitched in his sleep. There were flecks of grey in the black hair.

'Right, Jim,' Corrance said with obvious relief. 'I'll leave you to it.'

Bergerac nodded. Corrance left the cell. For a few seconds Bergerac stared down at the sleeping man. There was no hurry. He could remember what waking up after a bender was like.

He put a hand on Ferreira's shoulder, grimacing as a wave of stale beer hit his nostrils. He gave the shoulder a gentle shake.

'Alvaro? Alvaro?'

Ferreira stirred. His eyes opened and he caught sight of Bergerac. The eyes closed. The face muscles tightened. It reminded Bergerac of his daughter Kim as a toddler: she had been convinced that, when her eyes were closed, no one could see her.

'Come on, Alvaro. Time to wake up.'

Ferreira frowned. The eyes opened once more. He looked puzzled – almost as if he thought the name belonged to someone else.

'You're in a cell at police headquarters in Rouge Bouillon,' Bergerac said gently. 'I'm Detective Sergeant Bergerac.'

There was no mistaking the panic on Ferreira's face. He

stared at Bergerac with his mouth half open. Bergerac leant against the wall. He realized that he would have to take this slowly.

'Your name's Alvaro Ferreira?'

The little man nodded.

'A patrol car picked you up in Royal Square last night.' Bergerac's mouth twitched. 'You were throwing beer cans at the statue of George II. I'll need to see your papers — passport, work permit, that sort of thing. You're not a tourist, are you?'

Ferreira shook his head, wincing with pain. He cleared his throat. 'I am a waiter, sir.'

'Where?'

'It is called Lil's Place. A nightclub. Sir, I am sorry, I did not mean to get drunk. I – '

'OK.' Bergerac got to his feet. 'You'd better get up.'

The panic on Ferreira's face had turned to fear. 'Where will you take me, sir?'

'To Lil's Place.' Bergerac tried the effect of a smile. 'Don't worry. If Lil can vouch for you, there won't be much problem. Nothing very dreadful's going to happen.'

With those words, Bergerac realized later, he made his first mistake.

The Triumph Roadster came as a shock to Alvaro Ferreira.

Bergerac enjoyed his surprise; policemen weren't supposed to drive around in elderly sports cars.

It was a little after nine o'clock. The streets of St Helier were crowded with people going to work. Bergerac drove slowly out of necessity. It was a fine morning and surprisingly mild for December. He put the hood down, hoping that fresh cold air would complement the aspirins and black coffee that Ferreira had been given at police headquarters.

Lil's Place was one of the more successful nightclubs on

8

the island. This was due largely to the personality of its owner. At first sight, Diamanté Lil seemed to be decorative rather than forceful by nature – she was a mature blonde with a throaty laugh and more than her fair share of charm. But she was also an extremely shrewd businesswoman.

Bergerac knew another side of her. They had been friends for years – since the days when Lil had run the Royal Barge bar and restaurant on the St Aubin waterfront. She was one of the few friends who had stood by him when alcoholism, injury and the failure of his marriage came close to destroying his life.

He pushed the memories away. Now, thank God, it was easier to make the conscious effort to forget; the past laid fewer ambushes.

Ferreira stiffened as Bergerac manoeuvred the Triumph into a parking slot near Lil's flat.

'Cheer up,' Bergerac said. 'She won't eat you.'

As they waited outside the door Ferreira glanced nervously around. He barely came up to Bergerac's shoulder.

The door opened. Lil's face broke into a smile when she saw Bergerac. She was already up and dressed despite the fact she could not have got to bed before four o'clock.

Bergerac jerked his head at Ferreira. 'Is he one of yours?'

'Alvaro!' Lil seized Ferreira's arm and pulled him over the threshold. 'Have you been drinking again?'

Bergerac followed them into the flat. Lil took charge at once. She pushed Ferreira on to a sofa and poured him a cup of black coffee from the cafetière on the table. She left the room. A moment later she was back with a glass of water in which two Alka Seltzers were dissolving. She left the glass beside Ferreira and came over to Bergerac who was standing by the window.

'Does he do this often?' Bergerac asked quietly.

Lil shrugged. 'He's been working for me for nearly a month. This is the second time it's happened.'

9

'Papers all in order?'

She nodded. 'You want to see them? We'll have to go to my office.'

'Later, maybe.' Bergerac paused. 'Where was he before he came to you?'

'Oporto. He worked in a bar there.'

'He speaks good English for someone who's only been here a month.'

'Don't be so suspicious, Jim.' Lil squeezed his arm, taking the sting from her words. 'Always the copper. He learned from a cousin who used to work in London. What exactly happened?'

Bergerac explained.

'It won't mean much, will it?' Lil said. 'A fine, perhaps?'

'If that. He didn't do any damage.' Bergerac looked curiously at her. 'You sound worried.'

Lil shrugged. 'I am. Good waiters don't grow on trees. He's popular with the customers and Jean-Luc says he's honest. Anyway – I rather like him.'

Behind them the sofa creaked as Ferreira struggled to his feet.

'Madame,' he said. 'I am so sorry to bring this trouble to you.'

'Alvaro,' Lil said menacingly, 'there really will be trouble if you don't drink those Alka Seltzers.'

A few hours later Bergerac left the Bureau by a side entrance to lessen the risk of running into Detective Chief Inspector Barney Crozier.

His shift had another half-hour to run; Bergerac was playing truant. He felt no qualms about leaving before his time; he had cleared the urgent paperwork from his in-tray; and in any case he had arrived early – which was how he had come to be at the receiving end of Sergeant Corrance's exercise in buck-passing.

As he drove north out of St Helier his professional worries dropped away and his excitement increased. It had been a long time – over thirteen weeks. On an island measuring six miles by ten, few car journeys were lengthy; but this one seemed unbearably protracted.

At last he caught sight of the Channel, sparkling in the hard winter sunshine. It might have been draped in tinsel. Tinsel reminded him of Christmas and he felt a stab of panic. The shopping days to Christmas were down to single figures, and he hadn't even thought about presents.

He swung the car into a curving driveway lined with palm trees. Improbably trim lawns, broken only by neatly regimented trees and crisply defined flowerbeds, stretched away on both sides. As always, the gardens reminded Bergerac of a carefully tended municipal park.

The whitewashed Georgian house came into view. The Rolls was parked outside the converted stable block; there was no sign of Deborah's car. For an instant Bergerac wondered if his ex-wife had decided to deny him their daughter's company for a little longer.

Bergerac let the Triumph roll to a halt on the gravel sweep at the front of the house. The front door opened and Kim came running out. Bergerac felt a jolt of astonishment as he realized yet again that this young woman was his daughter; it seemed only a few months ago that she had been vandalizing her playpen.

After a few paces she slowed to a walk. Adult gravity settled over her like an ill-fitting coat. Bergerac repressed a smile. He got out of the car, ready to give her whatever sort of greeting she thought appropriate.

She hugged him like a child.

'Glad to be home?' he murmured into her hair.

'Yes. I wish – ' She broke off and moved away from him. 'Where are we going?'

Bergerac took the change of subject in his stride. 'Shall we have lunch out?'

He glanced at her and swiftly revised his intentions. Her clothes looked as if they had come from the nearest charity shop; but he was sufficiently aware of contemporary teen-age fashion to realize that Kim had made a special effort for the occasion.

'I thought perhaps La Capannina or La Tourelle.'

Her face was some compensation for the damage that either establishment would do to his bank balance.

'After all,' he went on, 'it's a celebration.'

But Kim was no fool. 'Are you sure we can afford it?'

He grinned at her. 'We'll manage.'

'I'll get my coat.'

They turned at the same moment to see Deborah standing in the doorway. Bergerac wondered how long she had been there. They exchanged greetings with the politeness that only the divorced can achieve. Kim went into the house.

'I'd like to have a chat sometime,' Deborah said quietly, 'about Kim's education.'

Bergerac raised his eyebrows. 'You want her to change schools? Again?'

He had argued against sending Kim to a boarding school in England, partly because he was by no means sure that he approved of private education; but more because it made it harder for him to see his daughter.

'Perhaps. A boarding school on Jersey might give her the best of both worlds.'

It would also mean Kim would have to be uprooted once more. Since her parents' divorce, she needed stability more than most children. Except she wasn't a child any longer.

'We'll talk about it later,' he said harshly.

There were heavy footsteps in the hall.

'Ah! Jim!' Charlie Hungerford, Deborah's father, was

wearing Wellington boots and carrying an armful of holly. 'Nice to see you. You should drop in more often.'

Bergerac was instantly suspicious. Hungerford oozed *bonhomie* for much the same reason as a skunk stank: for the purposes of personal survival.

'Have a drink while you're here. Not that you can call an orange juice a drink. Actually, I want a word with you. The Committee was discussing the arrests quota only the other day.'

The penny dropped. Hungerford had clawed his way to the chairmanship of the Law and Order Committee which was nominally responsible for overseeing the work of the States Police. Bergerac had heard rumours that some of the other Committee members were not entirely happy with their chairman. At a guess, Hungerford wanted to gather ammunition to defend his position.

Well, he wouldn't get any support from his former son-in-law.

'Ready, Dad?'

Bergerac nodded, grateful to be rescued. He opened the passenger door for Kim before he got into the car himself. Hungerford, still laden with holly, scuttled round to the driver's side.

'Why not stay to lunch?' he suggested. 'I'd like you to meet one of our guests. Could be useful to you. Interesting chap – might even get him on the Committee – '

Bergerac let out the clutch. The roar of the exhaust drowned the rest of Hungerford's words. Out of the corner of his eye he noticed that Kim was giggling.

'Poor Grandad,' she said. Their eyes met for an instant. 'Dad – what do you want for Christmas?'

'I don't know,' Bergerac said. 'What about you?'

'What I really want is a party.'

CHAPTER
2

Oliver was nervous.

He rang the airport and confirmed that the flight had landed on time. Maybe Quine had difficulty in getting a taxi; maybe the taxi had broken down; or maybe Quine had got off at the wrong place.

The minute hand on Oliver's watch had hardly moved since the last time he had looked at it. All he could do was wait. He had chosen a bar-restaurant in St John's, on the assumption that it was better that Quine should not come to the farmhouse. Perhaps that had been a mistake. Anyone might see them together. But on the other hand . . .

His thoughts circled round and round, looking for an exit that didn't exist. The ashtray filled up with Gauloise butts. The level in the Sancerre bottle dropped below the halfway mark.

'Oliver!'

He jumped as a hand clapped him on the shoulder.

'There you are!' the voice went on. 'Long time, no see.' The stranger raised the volume slightly for the barman's benefit. 'I'll have a large Scotch. Bell's, if you've got it.'

The voice belonged to London; the body belonged to a second-row rugby forward, run to seed. The face had a broken nose and a beaming smile.

As the barman moved away, the smile vanished.

'I thought you'd rather put this on first-name terms,' Quine said quietly. 'Less conspicuous. I'm Ronny.'

On first-name terms? How much does Quine know?

Oliver swallowed. 'How did you know . . .?'

'Who you were? It wasn't exactly difficult. I've been watching you from the other bar for a couple of minutes. Besides, my researcher dug up a photo of you.'

The whisky came. Quine steered Oliver to a table by the window. At this time of year the place was nearly empty.

'Nice place, Jersey,' Quine said. 'Know what? I could almost see myself living here.' He added with no discernible change of tone: 'I've got the detailed report here' – he tapped his briefcase – 'but right now a verbal briefing might be more productive.' He paused, licking his lips. 'For both of us, Oliver. For both of us.'

Oliver lit a cigarette. His hand trembled.

Quine smiled, revealing a jagged row of yellow teeth. 'There's nothing to worry about. You got a problem; I can help you solve it. It's as simple as that.'

'What do you mean?' Oliver said. The words came out more loudly than he had intended.

Quine was staring out of the window. A maroon sports car came up the road and passed the bar-restaurant. A man in a leather jacket was driving. Oliver caught a glimpse of a girl in the passenger seat.

'Nice motor,' Quine said. 'Triumph Roadster, eh? Must be thirty-five years old if it's a day. See the bit of skirt? Young enough to be his daughter.'

A waiter came over with a menu. Quine waved him away.

'All right,' he went on, 'no point in beating round the bush. Four tenders are being considered for the contract. The word is that there's little to choose between them. The Planning Committee will make the decision when it next meets.'

'I know that,' Oliver interrupted.

Quine ignored him. 'That's the theory. In practice the Committee doesn't count for much. But two people do –

the chairman, bloke named Littledean, and the Chief Planning Officer. The Committee generally approves the planning officer's recommendations. And on something as big as this, they'll listen extra hard to him. They don't want egg on their faces.'

Oliver nodded towards the briefcase. 'You've got dossiers on them? On the two that count?'

'Oh, yes. Spent a lot of time digging. I thought you'd want that.' Quine paused. 'In fact that's what you really wanted all along.'

'It's standard commercial practice,' Oliver said defensively.

'Of course it is. Anything to give the seesaw a tilt in the right direction. Knowledge is power, that's my motto. The thing is, knowledge by itself is useless. You have to act on it. Not so easy for you, is it? You're here on Jersey, but you need the action on the mainland, where Danston and Littledean are. And that's where I may be able to help. My firm has a lot of useful contacts.' Quine showed his teeth again. 'If "contacts" is the right word.'

Oliver toyed with the gold bracelet of his wristwatch. He realized that he was being manoeuvred into making a decision he didn't really want to make. Not yet. But Quine was right: he needed the professional expertise that Quine could offer. It was true that the man came highly recommended. But was he trustworthy?

Quine was looking at him. Oliver had the uneasy feeling that the private investigator knew precisely what was going through his mind.

'You haven't got much option, have you?' Quine said at last. 'According to my information, your back's up against the wall. You need that contract like you've never needed anything before. Well? Do we have a deal?'

*

16

At the same time a few miles away, Charlie Hungerford was uncorking a bottle of champagne.

He was in a good temper. Guy Pilsen-Smith was in many ways the ideal guest: he was wealthy; he was a self-made man who hailed from Hungerford's native Yorkshire; and he was a newcomer to Jersey, which meant that Hungerford had an edge over him in local society. Hungerford's definition of local society was a limited one: it included only those whose income and assets were on the same level as his own. The island had an area of roughly forty-five square miles; and there were approximately three millionaires for each square mile: *that* was local society.

'You got the house sorted out now?' Hungerford handed glasses to his guest and his daughter. 'Needed a lot of work, I imagine. Over the years it's been left to wrack and ruin.'

Pilsen-Smith sipped the champagne appreciatively. 'I like a challenge, Charlie. Meat and drink to me.'

'That's the place with a Martello tower, isn't it?' Deborah asked.

'That's right.' He turned towards her, his fleshy face creasing into a smile. 'I gather it's something of a rarity in the north of the island. Almost all of the others are on the south and east coasts, because that's where the beaches are.'

'Then why did they build one there?'

'To guard the inlet. It's small, but it's a natural harbour.' Pilsen-Smith grinned. 'The inlet's why I bought the house, in point of fact. Have to put my boats somewhere.'

Deborah politely asked about the boats. Pilsen-Smith went on at great length about his ocean-going yacht, his converted lifeboat and his cabin-cruiser. He had started his career in the Merchant Navy, and his interest in boats bordered on the obsessive. Deborah smothered a yawn.

They were sitting in the room that Hungerford called the library, though it was rare for anyone to read a book there.

17

A log fire smouldered with picturesque inefficiency in the grate; the real heat came from two radiators.

'Your son a sailor too?' Hungerford said.

Pilsen-Smith shrugged. 'Knows his way around a boat, I'll say that for him.'

Deborah sensed that he wanted to avoid the subject of his son. She said brightly, 'Do you plan to get involved in local politics, Mr Pilsen-Smith?'

'Call me Guy, please. Yes, it had crossed my mind. I believe in contributing something to the community.'

'Quite right,' Hungerford said. 'I'm on several committees myself.' He looked modestly into his drink. 'I think I can say I pull my weight.'

Pilsen-Smith nodded approvingly. 'In my view a hard-headed businessman is needed on every public committee. You tend to get too many makeweights. Do-gooders and hot-air merchants.'

'My point exactly, Guy!' Hungerford got to his feet in his excitement. 'If I've said it once, I've said it a hundred times. Cost-effectiveness, that's the bottom line. You identify priorities and you go for them. Well, it's common sense to you and me, but it's double Dutch to half my colleagues. You wouldn't believe some of the things I've heard on the Law and Order Committee.'

'I gather you're the chairman?'

Pilsen-Smith stood up and joined his host by the window. He was wearing a tweed jacket with a mustard check. With his pursed mouth, his plump body and his short, insignificant legs, he reminded Deborah of one of the goldfish in her father's ornamental pond.

'For my sins,' Hungerford said. 'You'd think it'd be simple enough to oversee the States Police. It would be, if I didn't have to deal with the bleeding hearts on the Committee.' He stared out of the window towards the Channel for a moment. Then he added, with a casual air that deceived no one, 'As a matter of fact, we may have a vacancy coming up in the New Year.'

'Someone said your' – Pilsen-Smith glanced in Debby's direction – 'former son-in-law is in the police. Do you find it helpful to have – ah – grass-roots contacts in the force?'

'Oh, yes,' Hungerford said easily. 'I've occasionally been able to point old Jim in the right direction. And of course it works both ways.'

Deborah blinked at this unusual description of the relationship between her father and Jim Bergerac. The clock on the mantelpiece struck one. She stood up gracefully.

'I think lunch will be ready.'

'Luncheon is served,' the waiter said.

He wasn't much older than Kim, but his solemnity was funereal. He had yet to learn that the average customer doesn't have much time for pompous waiters; he could have done with a few tips from Alvaro Ferreira. Bergerac guessed he wanted to be a butler when he grew up.

Kim repressed a giggle. The waiter led the way into the dining room. Bergerac brought up the tail-end of the little procession.

Both of them had mushrooms stuffed with garlic, breadcrumbs and parsley as their starters. As Kim had said: 'If we both have it, we won't be able to smell each other afterwards.'

After the third mushroom, she paused for a sip of wine.

'Dad?'

'Um?' Bergerac said with his mouth full.

'What d'you think about this party?'

'Seems a good idea.' Bergerac hesitated, aware that for some reason the subject was a delicate one. 'What does your mother say?'

Kim screwed up her face. 'She says she's too busy to

organize it, not at such short notice. But it wouldn't take much organization. Anyway, that's not the real problem.'

'Then what is?'

'My idea of a party isn't the same as hers and Grandad's.'

Bergerac grinned. 'Coca-Cola and paper hats? Chocolate buttons and Blind-Man's-Buff?'

Kim nodded. Suddenly she grinned back. 'It's not quite that bad. But you've got the right idea. They'd want to get a caterer in, and ask parents too. You know what they're like.'

There was a moment's silence. Bergerac could guess the sort of party Kim had in mind: a thumping disco, a display of mildly alcoholic drinks, a ton of crisps and above all the complete absence of intrusive adults. She wanted to be treated as a grown-up; Deborah and Hungerford still treated her as a child. Most normal families found it possible to work out a teenage compromise. But the Bergeracs were not a normal family.

'Tell me,' he said cautiously. 'Why is this so important to you?'

Kim put down her fork. 'I've lost touch with most of my friends here – you know, since I went to school on the mainland. After a while, you stop writing letters . . .' Her voice was tightly controlled, and Bergerac realized abruptly how difficult this admission was for her to make. 'If you're not around for most of the year, they tend to forget you. And it's so *boring* in that house with just Mum and Grandad for company.'

So that was it. Kim was lonely.

'Will you help?' Kim said.

Bergerac hesitated. 'I'll try. I promise you that.'

*

20

'It's worth a try, I suppose,' Oliver said.

'I promise you more than a try.' Quine stretched in the passenger seat of the Jaguar XJS. 'It's a virtual certainty.'

'How can you be so sure?'

'Relax, Oliver. Look, you phone Littledean this afternoon. I've already prepared the ground. Ask him to lunch early next week. Say you're a friend of Ronny's and he'll know what you mean. He's expecting you.' Quine belched happily. 'You'll have plenty to talk about. Littledean used to be a builder too – until he retired to devote all his energies to local government. You'll see: there'll be no problem.'

By now the airport was only a mile away. There was plenty of time before Quine's flight back to Heathrow. Oliver allowed the car to dawdle through St Peter's. He glanced at Quine, who looked the picture of well-fed contentment. *Well, so he should,* Oliver thought vindictively, *after a lunch like that and with the size of the cheque I gave him.*

'It's not Littledean who worries me,' he said. 'It's the other one. The planning officer.'

'Danston?' Quine chuckled. 'You leave John Danston to me. He's good at his job, but he's got personal problems. Everyone has their little weakness. Once you find it, you're home and dry. Just like Orwell's *1984.*'

Oliver frowned; an expensive education had failed to equip him to deal with literary allusions. 'I don't follow.'

'Orwell's hero tried to rebel against the system,' Quine said patiently. 'Against Big Brother. So Big Brother found out his weakness, which happened to be rats. After that the hero toed the line. See?'

Despite the warmth of the car, Oliver shivered. 'What will you do?'

'We'll talk about it next week, OK? We may need a little help at this end – nothing too difficult. Maybe a spot of baby-sitting.'

'*What?*'

Quine let another hundred yards slide by before he answered. 'Might be best if you did it yourself.'

'I don't know what you mean.'

'After you've met Littledean, you'll be coming up to London, right? You've got the address. We'll sort out the details then.'

'Why not now?'

'I need more information. Besides, I want to discuss the whole business with my associate before I go any further.'

'Is that wise?' Oliver licked his lips which had suddenly gone dry. 'I mean, the fewer people we involve, the better. Do you need to tell him?'

'Yes. We're a partnership, Oliver; we work better together. And by the way – it's not a him. It's a her.'

CHAPTER
3

At this time of year, the beach was nearly deserted.

It was a grey, blustery day and the tide was low. They had to walk fast along the line of the sea wall to keep warm. On their left St Ouen's Bay stretched away to the Atlantic Ocean.

Susan tucked her arm in Bergerac's. 'I've been thinking about Kim's party.'

Bergerac shrugged. 'It's no good, love. Debby might agree, but Charlie won't, not unless we play it his way. And that would be worse than useless as far as Kim's concerned.'

'I know. He treats her as if she's about ten.'

Her voice was bitter. Bergerac looked sharply at her.

Susan laughed without much amusement. 'It was the same when I was a kid. My dad thought my favourite food was ice-cream and jelly till I was about twenty-one. It was different for my brother, of course. Dad couldn't wait for him to grow up.'

'Charlie holds the purse-strings. You know that.'

'That doesn't make it any better.' Susan slowed their pace until they drifted to a halt. 'He's a fool – Kim won't thank him for it.'

'OK, so what do we do?'

'What about your flat? Charlie and Deborah couldn't object if you had Kim's party there.'

Bergerac sighed. 'I thought about that. But the flat's too

small. It's over-crowded with more than three people. And you know what the neighbours are like.'

'There's my place,' Susan said softly.

'But you don't want a horde of teenagers trampling – '

'Why not? Think about it, Jim. It's big enough. They can make all the noise they like.'

'Something might get broken.'

'I've had parties before. You just lock away your valuables.'

'It's a great idea,' Bergerac said. He stroked Susan's hair.

'"But" – go on, say it.'

'But Kim doesn't really know you. And Debby and Charlie might not be too happy.'

'Maybe it's about time Kim and I got to know each other better.' Susan hesitated. 'As for your . . . as for the Hungerfords, I know what they think of me. Susan Young, estate agent and qualified *femme fatale*. Jim's fancy woman in her St Helier love-nest.'

Bergerac squeezed her arm. 'That's their problem.'

'I know. But it shouldn't be Kim's as well. Jim, she *needs* that party.'

Bergerac ran his hand over her face. He had never really thought of Susan as a determined woman – though a weak-willed person wouldn't have held down her job for long.

'The way things are going,' he said slowly, 'I think Kim's going to get her party after all.'

Oliver felt happier than he had been for months.

He had not realized it would be so easy. Here they were in this perfectly charming Cotswold restaurant. The Châteaubriand had been superb. The second bottle of Burgundy had been even better than the first. He supposed he might be a little drunk, but in the most pleasant way possible; the alcohol seemed to have sharpened all his faculties.

He pushed the cheeseboard across the table. 'Have some of this Stilton, George. It really *melts* in the mouth.'

Littledean speared a segment on to his plate. 'It sounds very straightforward.' He had a voice like shingle moving under the waves. 'It is definite, isn't it?'

'Absolutely.' Oliver topped up their glasses. 'The Americans have already begun.'

'You won't mind me asking how you happen to know.'

Oliver leant forward. 'Between ourselves, it was originally going to be an Anglo-American takeover. We were interested in acquiring a Continental base and Saulieu Frères seemed ideal. And of course the asset-stripping would have been immensely profitable. But in the end the board decided the time wasn't right. At present we should be concentrating on Colton New Town.'

'But the takeover is going ahead?'

'Oh, yes. The Americans went in with a Swiss company. The shares have just begun to rise – only very slightly. Go in now, and you can expect a three or four hundred per cent profit. And that, of course, is just' – Oliver's eye fell on the menu that was open on the table – 'just the appetizer. This could be the start of a very profitable partnership.'

Littledean, mellowed by the meal, was in a receptive frame of mind. Yet he was no fool: his questions were shrewd and he required detailed answers. He wanted to be sure not only that his profits would be guaranteed; he also needed to be convinced that the deal would be untraceable.

Oliver ordered brandy and cigars with the coffee and set to work. The alcohol, he thought, made him both eloquent and reassuring. He knew he was good at discreet negotiations where much of the real bargaining was left unspoken; he had had a good deal of practice. He tried with increasing success to ignore what the Americans would do if they found out; it didn't bear thinking about.

At last Littledean nodded his heavy head. 'That seems quite straightforward. We've both got everything to gain and nothing to lose.'

Wrong, Oliver thought. *I've got everything to lose.*

Aloud he said: 'Will there be any problems at your end?'

Littledean's eyes narrowed. 'Depends what you mean by problems. Most of the committee will follow my lead. As long as Danston doesn't put a spoke in.'

'The Chief Planning Officer?'

'John Danston,' Littledean said, almost dreamily. 'Funny bloke. Intense – nervy, you might say. But he carries a lot of clout with the rest of the committee. Personally I can't stand the man, but that's neither here nor there. The snag is, he's the sort of chap who wouldn't ring his wife from the office phone because it was a personal call. You know, he'd sooner die than nick one of the rate-payers' envelopes.' Littledean sighed and added, more in sorrow than in anger: 'What can you do with a man like that?'

'Quine told me,' Oliver said.

'I can't handle Danston for you. You'll have to find some other way.'

Their eyes met. Oliver drew on his cigar.

'You can leave that side of things to me,' he said with a confidence he didn't feel. He tapped a cylinder of ash into the saucer of his cup. 'I've got Quine working on it. I'm meeting him this afternoon.'

Littledean dabbed his mouth with a napkin. 'Tell me,' he said quietly, 'how much does Ronny Quine know?'

'Only – ah – the broad outline.'

'It might be wiser to keep it that way.'

Oliver wondered if Littledean was trying to warn him. 'Do you know him well?'

26

'We go back a long time. I knew him when he was still in the Fraud Squad.'

'The Fraud Squad?' Oliver licked his lips. 'He didn't mention that. He told me he was a retired policeman but –'

'Retired?' Littledean grunted with laughter. 'That's a good one. Most people would say he was sacked.'

When Ronny Quine came back from the phone Norma Jean Veldman was washing the blood from her hands. The little basin, its enamel cracked and pitted by generations of use, was streaked with rust-coloured stains.

Jorge Ferreira was tied to a hard wooden armchair in the middle of the workshop. There wasn't much left of his face but the small, brown eyes were still alive. He looked imploringly at Quine and tried to say something. The swollen lips and broken teeth distorted the words, but the sense was clear enough.

There was blood on the concrete around the chair. Quine realized they would have to hose the floor before they left. It had been a messier business than he had anticipated. He was glad now that Norma Jean had insisted on using the former builder's yard he rented in Hounslow.

'That was Fatty Oliver,' Quine said.

Norma Jean dried her hands on a paper handkerchief and looked critically at her red nail varnish. 'How did it go?' she asked.

'He's over the moon. "The negotiations were completely satisfactory" – and that's a quote. Him and Littledean got on like a house on fire.'

'How much time have we got?'

Quine wandered over to the Cortina which he had parked just inside the big double doors. He opened the boot. Luckily, it was empty.

'He's driving up now,' he said. 'He phoned from Cheltenham. Won't be much more than a couple of hours.'

One thumbnail failed to pass the test. Norma Jean snapped open her handbag and found the nail varnish. Frowning with concentration, she touched up the offending nail.

Quine glanced at his watch. 'Plenty of time.'

She looked up. 'We'd better talk now. There may not be time later.'

'We take the job?'

'Of course we do,' she said impatiently. 'It's a paying proposition in any case. But now' – she jerked her head at Jorge – 'it's much more important. We need to go to Jersey and this job's the perfect cover. No risk of anyone seeing us arrive. No hotel registers. And if anything goes wrong we can always lean on Oliver.'

Quine lit a cigarette. 'OK, we've got a name and we've confirmed the Jersey rumour. But it may not be so easy to find him.'

Norma Jean closed her handbag. 'We've got something else to go on now.' Her eyes flicked across the room to the motionless figure in the chair. 'I had another go with the drill while you were on the phone. We'll need to get a list of Jersey nightclubs.'

'So he's still a waiter?'

'That's what Jorge thinks. Or he might be behind the bar. Definitely some kind of nightclub.'

'But – '

'For God's sake, Ronny,' she snapped. 'Stop raising objections. You'll find him. You're meant to be a private detective, aren't you? Just do as I say and it'll all be fine.'

She stroked his arm. Quine caught her hand and squeezed it gently. Jorge Ferreira was moaning behind them, but they might have been alone in the room.

'You'll see, Ronny,' she said softly. Abruptly she withdrew her hand. 'When we meet Oliver, I'll play hard to get, OK? I'll say that I'll only take the job if you come in on it too. And we don't want to seem too enthusiastic. It's bad for business.'

'If you say so.' Quine shrugged. 'Oliver's a fool and he's out of his depth. I reckon he'd believe anything we told him.'

'Don't underestimate him, Ronny. Come on, it's time we were moving.'

Norma Jean opened a drawer and pulled out a length of fine wire with wooden toggles at either end.

Jorge knew what was happening. He began to scream.

Norma Jean moved behind him. With one swift movement she whipped the wire round Jorge's neck. She twisted the toggles in a clockwise direction. She took her time about it.

'I'll tidy up here,' she said to Quine, 'and drive up to the flat afterwards.'

As Norma Jean tightened the garrotte, the screams forced her to raise her voice.

'Put him in the boot of the Cortina,' she went on, 'and dump it in the long-stay car park at Heathrow. If I were you, I'd come back by tube.'

The screaming had stopped. Jorge clawed at his neck.

'The car should be safe enough for a few hours. I doubt if the owner knows it's been stolen.'

The hands fell away from the neck. Jorge fell forward, his limbs straining against the luggage ties which pinned him to the chair. Norma Jean continued to twist the toggles.

Quine frowned and looked away.

'By the way,' Norma Jean said. 'As far as Oliver's concerned, I'm Marilyn. OK?'

Emma Danston had once been a perfect secretary. Now she tried equally hard to be a perfect wife.

It was not that she was subservient by nature – quite the reverse was true. But if she made a decision, she liked to carry it through; if she took on a job, she liked to do it properly. She was not a woman who believed in half measures.

As a secretary, she had derived a wry pleasure from controlling the men who were supposed to be her bosses. But the pleasure had palled, perhaps because it was so easily won. Approaching thirty, she had decided that it was time to marry and have a family. If she left it much longer it might be too late.

She thought about it carefully and decided to marry John Danston. At the time she was working for him, so she already knew him far better than many wives ever know their husbands. She knew that John had a lot of problems. But he also had a secure, reasonably well-paid job; he was conscientious to the point of quixotism; and he was one of the few genuinely good men she had ever met. Goodness was an old-fashioned virtue but, as a clergyman's daughter, Emma had been brought up to appreciate it. And there was another point in his favour that, rational though she was, she could hardly ignore. She happened to be in love with him.

Six months later they were married. Emma had never seriously regretted the decision, though occasionally she wished that life with John could be a little more exciting. It would be nice if, out of the blue, he would sweep her off for a dirty weekend in Bermuda – or anywhere else for that matter; it was the principle that counted. But with John everything had to be mapped out well in advance: she even knew precisely what Christmas presents she would be getting this year because John disliked making speculative choices and believed in full consultation.

She heard his key turning in the front door and got up, with a sudden rush of pleasure, to greet him. Their house was on a well-designed modern estate, which had been sited with convenience in mind: it was convenient for the motorway, two large provincial shopping centres and all the rural amenities that their part of England had to offer. Emma liked the house; John thought it was a good investment.

He came into the big sitting room and laid his briefcase on the bureau. She knew at once that it had been a bad day. The vertical lines between his eyebrows were more noticeable than they had been at breakfast, and his eyes were tired. He looked as though he had lost a battle he hadn't expected to win.

They kissed. John made a break with routine and hugged her. She sensed that he was more than usually glad to be home.

Emma pushed him gently towards an armchair. She poured him a small whisky with a lot of water and gave herself a glass of sherry. Routine could be reassuring at times like this.

He took the drink with a smile of thanks. 'Everything OK?'

That too was routine.

She nodded and sat down on the floor beside his chair. For a few minutes they sat, sipping their drinks, in a comfortable silence.

'Have you had a rough day?' Emma said at last. It was not really a question.

'It's those Colton New Town tenders,' he said. 'They mean a hell of a lot of work. And I've had Littledean breathing down my neck again. Morning *and* afternoon.'

She twisted her head so she could see him. 'You need a break.'

'There's no time. What I really need is a bit of peace and quiet at the office. Someone's always interrupting. I just can't concentrate.'

'You've got a deadline to meet?'

He passed a hand over his forehead. 'I need to get it sorted out by the Christmas break.'

The hint of panic in his voice alarmed her even more than the lines on his face. She knew how worries built up in his mind until the fragile barrier of his control could no longer withstand the pressure. Once, before their marriage, she had seen what could happen when the control gave way.

'Why don't you bring the tenders home?' she suggested. 'You'd work much more efficiently. Ned Arlen wouldn't mind.'

Arlen was the County Council's chief executive. He appreciated both the vulnerability and the expertise of his Chief Planning Officer. Emma had found him a useful ally in the past.

John stirred in his chair. 'I could do that, I suppose.'

His tone blended lack of enthusiasm with a touch of embarrassment. Emma knew the reasons for both. It irritated her momentarily that he was so frightened of hurting her feelings.

'I've got an idea,' she said carefully. 'You work at home. We'll go off for a few days so you'll be alone. There's plenty of food in the freezer – you'd hardly have to do anything. You'll be able to get the tenders out of the way. And afterwards we can have a proper Christmas.'

'But where would you go?'

'Southampton. You remember the bed-and-breakfast we stayed at, the summer before last? They're sure to have vacancies at this time of the year.'

'You'd be bored,' he said. 'And you must have lots to do at home.'

He was weakening, Emma thought. She patted his leg.

'When have you ever known me to be bored? And I've done most of the preparations for Christmas. We'd be fine, John. If you would.'

His hand found hers. 'I'd miss you.'

'We'd miss you.' She returned the pressure of his fingers.

'But it would be worth it. We could have a proper Christmas. If you're worried about work, it won't be much fun for any of us.'

They talked about it for a few minutes more. John put up only a token resistance. Emma clinched the matter by phoning Southampton. Two rooms were available and the landlady would be delighted to have them.

As she returned from the phone, Emma bent down and kissed the small bald patch on his head.

'That's settled, darling,' she said. 'If we stayed, I'd only worry about you.'

She would worry about him wherever they were. It wasn't much more than twenty-four hours later that she realized that she was worrying about the wrong person.

CHAPTER
4

'Deputy Hungerford is here to see you, sir.'

Detective Chief Inspector Crozier, safe in the knowledge that he was alone in his office, rolled his eyes. Peggy sounded harassed over the intercom; his secretary's voice was usually calm and well-modulated. He couldn't blame her. And he could hardly blame her for ignoring his orders that he wasn't to be disturbed for anything less than an Act of God. Hungerford qualified as an Act of God. No other explanation of his existence was possible.

Crozier glanced up at the clock on the wall. It was late in the afternoon. He had another dozen files in his in-tray. He had been hoping to skim through them quickly and get home at a reasonable time. For once.

But the best-laid plans of policemen had the habit of going awry when Charlie Hungerford was on the scene. Crozier had the usual copper's distrust of politicians. Hungerford had been bad enough when he was a mere member of the public. As a deputy in the States, Jersey's legislative assembly, and chairman of the Law and Order Committee he was insupportable. But he was also uncomfortably influential.

Crozier punched the button on his intercom, remembering just in time that Hungerford would be able to hear what he said. 'Yes, of course, Peggy. Please send him in.'

Hungerford burst into the office. 'Good of you to see me at such short notice, Barney. I know how busy you are.'

Crozier gave his guest a chair.

'I've just come from the Committee meeting,' Hunger-ford went on. 'We had quite a discussion about the arrests quota. In my view it's an excellent yardstick of police efficiency – '

'Yes, but – ' Crozier began.

' – because it's solid statistical evidence of success.' Hungerford paused. 'Or failure. I mean, you can't argue with the figures, can you?'

Hungerford sounded as if he was quoting himself; he had probably used exactly the same words to the Committee, half an hour earlier. Crozier murmured something about prevention rather than cure being an important aspect of a policeman's job.

'That's not the point!' Hungerford said.

'But surely – '

'The point is,' Hungerford swept on, 'we're discussing departmental allocations for the next financial year. Now, the arrests quota is down for the last quarter. A number of people on my Committee are arguing against expanding police resources. They're saying that in real terms the crime rate's dropping. That the police don't need the money. And that other departments do.'

'The quota's always down in winter,' Crozier said. 'Tourism's seasonal, we all know that. And the Bureau's quota drops more than CID's or uniformed branch's. It's what you'd expect.'

'It's what *you'd* expect,' Hungerford snarled. 'It's what *I'd* expect. It's what anyone with an ounce of intelligence would expect. But you try telling it to some of my Committee.'

The pieces fitted together in Crozier's mind. He felt an unwilling admiration for Hungerford's deviousness. The bluster was misleading; the man could have given Machia-velli a few tips.

The problem was political. Hungerford and his allies on

the Committee had a traditional view of law and order —
and they were prepared to fight to maintain and increase
the States' allocation to the police force. But some Committee members were less concerned about law and order: in a
caring society, they thought, the police should be a sort of
investigative sub-section of the social security department.

Crozier knew he was oversimplifying the matter; but he
had the essentials right. He also knew that the chairman's
position was by no means the sort of job you held for life. If
Hungerford were muscled out, his successor might be even
worse, from Crozier's point of view.

Better the devil you know?

The arrests quota had somehow become a political hot
potato in the middle of the row. If the quota went down, so
might Hungerford and the annual States Police allocation.
If it went up, his position and the allocation were corre-
spondingly strengthened.

'Well?' Hungerford was watching him closely. 'Do you
think we can push up the arrest quota in the next few
months?'

Yes, Crozier thought, *better the devil you know* . . .

'I can't promise anything, Mr Hungerford,' Crozier said
slowly. 'But we usually get a rise in the quota over the
Christmas period. And — as it happens — I have been
planning to review the Bureau's arrest procedures. It's been
in my mind for some time. Of course, if my colleagues in
CID and Uniformed were doing the same thing, I'd have
all the more reason to do so.'

The question mark dangled unobtrusively on the end of
the last sentence.

Hungerford nodded. 'Interesting. Life's full of coinci-
dences, eh?'

Crozier frowned. 'Sorry — you've lost me.'

'Nothing to worry about.' Hungerford grinned. 'It's just
that I had a word with your opposite numbers about the

arrests quota. This morning, it was. And they said much the same as you.'

Bergerac spent a frustrating couple of hours combing the streets of St Helier.

By the time he had finished he was no nearer achieving his aim than he had been at the start of the afternoon. Christmas presents resolutely refused to suggest themselves. He had seen a bracelet that Susan might like, but it was far too expensive. He had found a tape that he remembered Kim raving about; but he also remembered that she'd bought it already.

He was surprised to see a light in his living-room window as he approached his flat. He forgot his weariness immediately. Unannounced callers were rare. Bergerac could think of several people who might like to pay him an unwelcome impromptu visit.

He hesitated outside his front door. The thought crossed his mind that it might be wise to check with his neighbour before going in.

Then he heard a burst of laughter.

It could only be characterized as girlish giggling. Susan and Kim were there.

The adrenalin seeped away, leaving Bergerac feeling weary, foolish and, if the truth were told, a little irritable. He unlocked the door and went in.

Kim and Susan were side by side on the sofa, their heads bent over a book of brain-teasers. Susan nearly always had one of them in her handbag. It was a hobby that Bergerac had little time for; he reckoned that his working life presented him with enough puzzles.

'If Mr Green was mowing Mrs Black's lawn at 3.45,' Kim was saying, 'he couldn't have been digging up Mr Brown's dahlias at 3.50. Hello, Dad.'

Susan looked up and flashed him a smile. 'But Miss

Scarlet couldn't either,' she said, 'because one of the three women was planting courgettes at 3.45 and it must have been her, because we know what Mrs Black and Mrs Harebell were doing at that time.'

'So it must have been a man!' Kim said. 'Your neighbour let me in. You don't mind, do you, Dad? Then Susan saw the light and she dropped in too.' She glanced back to the book on her lap. 'How about Mr Burgundy? His garden's only two minutes away from Mr Brown's.'

'I'm going to make some tea,' Bergerac said to no one in particular.

He wandered into the little kitchen and put on the kettle.

A moment later, Susan joined him.

'What's up with you?' she asked in a low voice.

Bergerac put an arm round her shoulders. 'I suppose I felt excluded. Was is so obvious?'

'To me. Maybe not to Kim. But I wouldn't bank on it — she's bright.'

'Those damn puzzles,' Bergerac said. His annoyance was only half feigned.

'Cut it out, Jim,' Susan said. 'It's not easy for Kim and me to relate to one another. I'm not even a stepmother or something. Any common ground we can find is worth holding on to.'

'Sorry.' Bergerac let her go. 'Christmas shopping warps the personality. Especially when you can't find anything to buy.'

The kettle boiled. He made the tea while Susan set the tray. In the living room Kim was pencilling in the answer to the puzzle.

'It was Mr Grey,' she said triumphantly. 'Dad, has Susan told you?'

'Told me what?' Bergerac wondered if the conversation in the kitchen had been audible in here.

'About the disco. You know, the music and the lighting.

A friend of Susan's would do it for half price. He's a real professional, too. We've got it all sorted out, even where we get the glasses. It's all down to whether Mum and Grandad will agree.'

Susan was over by the window. She paused in the act of drawing the curtains. Outside the trees were bucking in the wind. A shower of rain rattled on the windowpane. She shivered.

'It's going to be a real storm tonight. I'm glad I'm not at sea.'

The *Star of Bethlehem* slid into the trough of another wave.

Oliver checked the Seafix radio direction-finder. No problem there. It was all under control. His oilskins were dripping with spray but he was still reasonably warm and dry.

The weather was an advantage: less risk of interference. He would have liked some coffee and a cigarette, but he couldn't trust either of the others with the helm. Bloody landsmen.

Marilyn was being sick again. Feeling pleasantly superior to such frailties, Oliver studied her rear view. She was swathed in oilskins; but imagination and memory could cope with that between them. He carried a lot of weight himself, and he liked his women to be on the voluptuous side. And she was blonde, too – another point in her favour; who cared if the colour came out of a bottle? Perhaps on Jersey they might get to know each other better. Presumably she was with Quine in more senses than one. He would have to be careful.

But in Oliver's present mood, Quine seemed insignificant. Just a fixer, really; not a doer. And what was he? A bent ex-copper turned seedy private eye. Marilyn would have to be mad to stay with him when she could have Oliver.

He realized she had finished. She moved slowly towards him, clutching for supports for both hands.

'Are you sure this boat's safe?' She had to scream to be heard over the storm. She bent closer to him; he could feel her breath on his face. 'It's so *small*.'

'Don't worry,' he shouted back. 'This old tub can handle anything. She's designed for bad weather, after all.'

Marilyn slipped and grasped his arm. He thought he heard her say, 'I wish I could believe you.'

'How about a cup of coffee,' he yelled. 'And a cigarette?'

He felt her shudder.

'Oh, Christ, no.'

For a moment he thought she was going to be sick again. She couldn't have much left to lose by now.

'What about Ronny?' he said. 'Couldn't he make some?'

'He's in a bloody coma.'

'Are the others OK?'

'Who cares?'

The *Star of Bethlehem* slid sideways without warning. Marilyn shrieked. Oliver pulled the helm over and the boat righted herself.

'I thought,' he went on, 'maybe that woman could make me some coffee . . .'

'For God's sake!' Marilyn shouted. 'They're rolling round the cabin floor. They're dead to the world.'

Far away, a bell was ringing.

Maybe it wasn't a bell. It could be a musical electric drill. Or one of those Black and Decker tools that whined away in every garden and garage during the summer. Or a persistent bird whose song he had never heard. Or a telephone.

He clung to the dream. It was warm there. He was lying on soft white sand with Emma. The sea was an impossible blue and there were palm trees along the shoreline.

The bell – or was it a boat's engine? You'd expect a boat on the sea.

They must be in the West Indies. He knew Emma wanted to go there. He had seen a tour operator's leaflet in her desk last week, while he was looking for the stapler. It was really surprisingly cheap at this time of year.

The bell rang on.

Well, why not? Once the Colton New Town business was out of the way. He had some leave due. They could afford it, just about. It would be a surprise for Emma. Now that would surprise her – not so much going to the West Indies as him surprising her.

Oh God, it *was* the telephone.

John Danston jerked upright. His mind was foggy – not just with sleep; he had taken a sleeping tablet before going to bed and a tranquillizer a few hours before that. His hand shot out to the other side of the bed. There was nothing beneath the duvet except a cool sheet.

Of course – Emma was in Southampton.

Danston groped for the light switch, knocking over his glass of water. Panic bubbled inside him. An accident? He had to answer that phone before it stopped ringing. The illuminated figures of the digital clock said 03.45.

The light blinded him.

He picked up the phone.

'Mr Danston?' It was a man's voice. He didn't recognize it. 'Mr Danston?'

'Yes – what is it?'

'You'll be glad to hear your nearest and dearest are safe and well. We'll be in touch in the morning.'

There was a click. The line went dead.

CHAPTER
5

'Excuse me. I want to report a kidnapping.'

Bergerac swung round. The uniformed desk sergeant was peering round the vast Christmas tree beside the counter, searching for the source of that small, breathless voice.

Crozier, who had cornered Bergerac on the other side of the Christmas tree, broke off in mid-sentence.

The boy hardly came up to the top of the counter. He was about six or seven, Bergerac thought; he noted automatically the freckled, earnest face, the red anorak and the blue jeans. The boy's left arm was in a sling and he was biting his lip.

Bergerac squatted down. 'Who's been kidnapped?'

The boy swallowed. 'I have.'

Bergerac glanced up at Crozier. 'Maybe this'll improve the quota.'

Crozier made a noise like a pressure cooker emitting steam.

At that moment the double doors opened. A gust of cold air swept into the reception area of the Bureau des Etrangers. Bergerac turned. A man and a woman hesitated on the threshold. Then the woman saw the boy and surged towards him. She engulfed him in her arms.

'There you are, Matthew! We thought we'd lost you.'

The boy tried to wriggle away. The colour had faded from his face, leaving the freckles like islands in a sea of pallor.

Probably in shock still, Bergerac thought. The sling and

the bandage beneath looked spotlessly clean – which suggested that the injury must have been recent; a kid that age would get grubby in no time at all.

'What's all this about?' Crozier demanded.

No one answered his question.

The woman allowed the boy to pull away. She was a well-upholstered blonde in her late thirties – attractive enough if you liked the brassier sort of barmaid. The accent was suburban London. To judge by her jewellery, she wasn't exactly poor.

She patted Matthew's head. 'Thank God we've found you.'

It was impossible to question the sincerity in her voice. There were tiny beads of sweat on her forehead, and her eyes were anxious. The fear had been genuine. Having children gave the meaning of fear an entirely new dimension. Bergerac could sympathize.

But clearly Crozier could not. 'Will someone tell me what's happening? Is that too much to ask?'

'Oh, I am sorry,' the woman said, glancing from Bergerac to Crozier, and then back to the boy; she threw just a touch of helplessness into that look. 'What's he been saying now?'

Bergerac cleared his throat. 'He's just told us he's been kidnapped.'

'Oh, Matthew! Not again. You mustn't waste people's time like this. Especially policemen.' She smiled at Bergerac and Crozier. 'I'm so sorry, really I am. He's always making up these stories. Honest, I don't know what to do with him sometimes. Lives in a world of his own. I blame it on the telly, myself.'

'Come on, Matt,' the man said; he was a few years younger than the woman and carried rather more flab than he needed. 'Be a good boy and say you're sorry.' He took

43

the boy's shoulders and shook him gently. 'Come on, for Mummy's sake.'

The boy stared at the Christmas tree. His face was blank.

'For Mummy's sake,' the man repeated.

His voice was slightly more up-market than the woman's. That was odd: with most couples it was the other way round. Susan had a theory that women cared more about the nuances of accent that bedevilled the British class system. Like all theories, there were exceptions to prove the rule.

Matthew's face tightened, as if he was fighting back tears. But he held them back and apologized to the police for wasting their time. The couple, obviously relieved, towed their son towards the door.

'You here on holiday?' Bergerac said.

'Yeah, one of these winter breaks.' The woman grinned. 'Didn't realize it'd be quite so cold, this time of year. Still, the shops are great.'

The man pulled open the door. 'Come on, we're late.'

Late for what? Bergerac wondered.

'Have a good holiday,' he said.

The doors swung shut behind them.

'Bloody kids!' Crozier muttered. 'If it's not one thing it's another.' He turned back to Bergerac. His voice hardened. 'Now look, Jim, as I was saying, you must have some sort of influence over Charlie Hungerford – '

'I doubt if Charlie thinks so.'

Bergerac spoke absently. He was staring through the glass panels of the door. The tourists climbed into a red Rover and drove away. The car had a Jersey numberplate; and the registration looked the same as Susan's office phone number, though it was difficult to be sure at this range. The door jamb blocked his view of the lefthand end of the numberplate, so he couldn't see if the registration was preceded by the 'H' that distinguishes hired cars on Jersey.

'But the point is, you know him personally,' Crozier snapped. He paused and glared at the desk sergeant. 'Haven't you got work to do?'

The sergeant hastily opened a file and seized a pencil. Bergerac noticed that the file was upside-down.

'Come into my office,' Crozier said. 'Too many flapping ears in this place.'

He led the way down the corridor. Crozier's fraying temper puzzled Bergerac. The Chief Inspector was not the calmest of men, but today he seemed exceptionally irritable. It couldn't just be the arrests quota – the Committee in general and Hungerford in particular were always going on about that; a simple statistic, however misleading, was something they thought they could understand.

Crozier waited until Bergerac had shut the office door behind him. He waved Bergerac to a chair.

'This time it's not just the arrests quota,' he said.

'But you said – '

'I know what I said. Look, Jim, it's more complicated than that. I had Hungerford in here yesterday. In a right state. The departmental allocations for the next financial year are up for discussion. And Hungerford's position is shaky: he might get pushed out of the chair.'

Bergerac grinned. 'That sounds like good news to me.'

'Well, it's not.' Crozier picked up a pencil and jabbed it, point downwards, at his blotter to emphasize what he was saying. 'Hungerford as good as said that, if he goes, our allocation will be pegged at last year's level or even cut. And the Bureau will be the first to feel the pinch.'

'That doesn't surprise me.'

Bergerac knew as well as Crozier that the Bureau was the newest and the most vulnerable of the police depart-

45

ments. CID had been lobbying for a merger – or rather a hostile takeover – ever since the Bureau had been founded.

Crozier seemed to read his mind. 'If Hungerford goes, we'll probably get Le Veillac in the chair. And you know what he and his mates are like.'

Deputy Le Veillac had been a stern critic of police methods and expenditure in the past. He was known to favour the merger lobby; and he believed that both departments were far too large for an island the size of Jersey.

Bergerac shrugged. 'I take your point. But how does the arrests quota fit in?'

'Politicians aren't logical. Le Veillac and Hungerford are fighting a battle. The arrests quota just happens to be the battlefield.'

'There's not much we can do except sit on the sidelines,' Bergerac said. 'What does Charlie want us to do? Create a crime wave for him? And then sort it out so the quota goes up?'

'Something like that. The Committee knows as well as we do that winter's a slack time for the Bureau. This isn't the mainland, thank God.' Crozier drew a frowning face on the blotter. He scored it out with a cross. 'But I did wonder if it might be worth you having a word with Hungerford – '

'Me? Come off it, Barney.'

'A discreet word, of course. In the family, as it were. Just try and head him away from the quota. You know, explain how inaccurate it is as a yardstick. You know the sort of thing.'

'Get them to choose another battlefield?'

Crozier nodded. 'That's it. Exactly. But do it tactfully – I mean, Hungerford's got our support. If there's any way we *can* help – where are you going, Jim?'

Bergerac had stood up. He looked down at Crozier, choosing his words with care.

46

'I'm sorry, Barney,' he said. 'But this stinks. It's political. I'm not talking to Charlie about this. If I can help it, I don't talk to him at all.'

Crozier said nothing.

Bergerac closed the door very quietly behind him. If Crozier had spoken, he would have slammed it.

A few years ago the anger he felt would have erupted into violent words or actions.

But things were different now. Since Bergerac had stopped drinking and got clear of a failed marriage, he had learned the value of control. Shouting at Crozier wouldn't have helped; nor would slamming the door.

But the anger was still there. Barney should have known him better. Damn it, he was a policeman, not a bureaucratic sycophant. Doing private deals with a member of the Law and Order Committee just wasn't his style. Particularly when the member in question was Charlie Hungerford.

He glanced at his watch as he reached the reception area. Two hours to go before he went off duty. The prospect did not please him: the Christmas presents still had to be bought; he would rather be at work than trailing round the shops.

The desk sergeant looked up as he passed. A paperback crime novel was partly concealed beneath the open file.

'So you're still in one piece,' he said jovially. 'What's bugging Crozier?'

Bergerac spread his hands out, feigning ignorance. It was one thing to tell Crozier to go to hell – but quite another to broadcast the details to the rest of the world.

'Can't take the responsibility.' The sergeant shook his head. 'I always said they shouldn't have made him up to Chief Inspector.'

Any organization had its backbiters. Bergerac had no desire to join them. He tried to change the subject.

'What's that?'

He pointed at a key-ring which lay on the counter. There was nothing on it except a brass .303 cartridge case, which acted as the tag.

'Eh? Oh, that. It belonged to the kid.'

'The kidnap victim?'

The sergeant laughed. 'Yeah, I think so. I found it in the tub the tree's in. It wasn't there before. Must've slipped out of his pocket.'

Bergerac picked up the key-ring and weighed it in his hand. It was cool and smooth to touch. Military memorabilia fascinated small boys. As a kid, he'd had a huge collection himself. Pride of place had gone to the German bayonet . . .

'They'll be back,' the sergeant said comfortably.

'You think so? They're just visitors. Maybe they're leaving today. The bloke was in a hurry to get somewhere.'

'Ah, well. That's his look-out.'

If the interview with Crozier hadn't taken place, Bergerac might have tossed the key-ring on to the counter and strolled out of the Bureau. But he was still angry – with Crozier and with himself.

'I'll take it if you want,' he said. 'I think I got their car number. I reckon it must be a hire car – should be easy to trace.'

Returning lost property to visiting children was a lot more wholesome than conducting slightly unsavoury negotiations with Charlie Hungerford.

The desk sergeant grinned. 'I thought Crozier said the computer should only be used in cases – '

'Ah, come on, George,' Bergerac said. 'It's Christmas.'

*

> God rest ye merry, gentlemen
> Let nothing ye dismay . . .

The music filtered through from the kitchen. He had put the radio on hours ago, hoping it would distract him. Emma had tuned to a local station. At this time of year every commercial seemed to be accompanied by a Christmas carol.

The music decreased in volume. The man who did the voice-over had a mid-Atlantic accent. *Presents for all the family at super, super prices – and super savings too!*

Danston put his head in his hands. The tranquillizers had clouded his mind. What family? He had rung the Southampton lodging-house, only to find out that they weren't there. According to the landlady, Emma had phoned to cancel the booking.

It didn't make sense. Nor did that phone call in the middle of the night. But maybe he had dreamed the phone call.

Another commercial – with 'Jingle Bells', this time, and a woman's voice saying, *Only a phone call away – own your own Pilsen home* . . .

Perhaps he should ring the police.

No – they'd laugh at him. They knew all about him at the local station. No one would believe him. They'd touch their heads and smile in the police canteen.

And of course it might have been a dream. Not so long ago, he often had dreams like that. He called them dreams – the word made them sound harmless and natural. Everyone had dreams.

The phone rang. He reached it on the second ring. Now was this part of the dream?

'Danston.'

There was a chuckle on the other end. 'Sleep well, John? Your nearest and dearest did.'

No, Danston thought, this couldn't be real; it was too bizarre. He must be imagining it. As long as he held on to that, as long as he could distinguish between reality and delusion, he couldn't be going mad.

'If anyone asks,' the voice went on, 'your wife thinks she might extend her holiday over Christmas. But don't go talking to people, will you, John? There's no need. And they might get the wrong idea. They might think your old trouble was coming back.'

'No,' Danston said quickly. 'I don't want to talk to anyone.' *And least of all to voices in my head.* 'Except Emma. I want Emma to come home.'

'So she will, John. Don't you fret. After the next meeting of the Planning Committee.' The rough, male voice was so soothing it might have been dipped in honey. 'Just do as I say and everything will be all right.'

He had to humour them, Danston realized; that way he retained the edge.

He cleared his throat and said aloud, 'I'll do whatever you say. I promise.'

CHAPTER
6

'Telephone, Jim.'

'Thanks, Peggy.'

Crozier's secretary covered the mouthpiece with her hand as she passed the handset to Bergerac.

'Not your favourite person, I'm afraid.'

Bergerac grinned at her. Peggy Masters seemed reserved and matronly on first meeting – especially since the death of her husband. But he had gradually come to realize that she had a wry and frequently irreverent sense of humour. With her job, she needed it – acting as a buffer state between Crozier and the rest of the world was not the easiest of tasks.

As he took the phone, Peggy murmured a name. Bergerac grimaced.

'Hello, Charlie,' he said. 'And what can I do for you?'

'Jim! Where've you been? I've been trying to get hold of you for hours.' The voice on the other end was a familiar blend of one part Yorkshire to two parts exasperation.

'Working, Charlie.' Bergerac could guess what this was about: the damned arrests quota. 'You know, it's what some people have to do to earn a living.'

Hungerford ignored the jibe. 'Well, never mind that. What's all this about you promising Kim a party? A disco? At her age?'

Bergerac switched his mental gears. 'She's sixteen, Charlie, in case you hadn't realized. And she's not Peter Pan either.'

'She's not old enough to be mixing with the likes of Susan Young.'

That was plain speaking with a vengeance. Bergerac kept a tight rein on his temper. His pride wasn't at issue – or even Susan's. The important thing was Kim's party.

'I'll give her a party,' Charlie went on. 'Damn it, this is her home. She can have the works, eh? I won't stint her. We'll hire outside caterers and send out proper invitation cards. We'll – '

'Charlie,' Bergerac interrupted. 'I've talked to her. She doesn't want that sort of party.'

'Well, what does she want?' Hungerford sounded hurt. 'I've done everything for that girl, Jim.'

That was true enough, Bergerac thought. Hungerford had helped to drive a wedge between her parents; he had tried to spoil Kim from the start; he prevented her from seeing her father whenever possible.

But the matter called for diplomacy. An open row would help no one, least of all Kim.

'Why don't we meet and talk about it?' Bergerac said. 'Er – discuss all the angles.'

He could almost hear the wheels whirring in Hungerford's mind. Charlie had no qualms about mixing his private and public concerns. He would be weighing up the possibility of backing down over Kim's party in return for the Bureau's cooperation in the little matter of the arrests quota. Bergerac was content to let him think that way. For the moment.

'Not a bad idea,' Hungerford said at last. 'As it happens, I'll be in St Helier this evening, at Lil's Place.' He coughed modestly. 'She wants my advice on something. Can you be there around 10.30?'

'OK.'

Bergerac put down the phone and passed a hand across his forehead, wiping imaginary sweat from his brow.

Peggy smiled primly.

'Any messages while I was out?'

'Constable Goddard was looking for you,' Peggy said.

'Thanks. I'll go and find him.'

'Try the canteen.'

Peggy's information was as accurate as usual. Barry Goddard was hunched over a cup of coffee in a corner of the police canteen. He was a slim, dark man who was more ambitious than he seemed. Bergerac reckoned he stood a good chance of being made up to detective sergeant in the next batch of promotions.

He looked up as Bergerac approached. 'I didn't realize we'd hit the big time. The Case of the Missing Key-ring.'

'Any luck?'

'The number belongs to a red Rover 2300.'

'A hire car?'

Goddard shook his head. 'Registered to Guy Pilsen-Smith, Old Highcliff Farm, St John's.'

'I know. I used to play up there when I was a kid.'

In memory it was a tumbledown place – on the coast, as the name implied. No doubt it had been renovated by now. Derelict houses were hard to find on Jersey.

Goddard took a sip of coffee and screwed up his face. 'What's our interest, Jim? It's not just the key-ring, is it?'

'Why not?' Bergerac said blandly. 'Probably means a lot to that kid.'

'Does the chief know about this?'

Bergerac sidestepped the question. 'You know that Barney Crozier likes the Bureau to have a caring public image. Thanks. Enjoy your coffee.'

He walked back to his office. Goddard was shrewd, no question of that. He was right – it wasn't just the key-ring. There was another point – something so small and subjective that Bergerac would have liked to be able to ignore it. It was certainly nothing that would justify the official interest of the Bureau. Crozier would say he was wasting valuable police resources.

And maybe Crozier would be right. All that Bergerac had to go on was the suggestion of a discrepancy; not even a discrepancy – more a sense of unease.

Put into words, it seemed absurd. Kids and parents usually fitted together, though not necessarily in terms of physical appearance; but Matthew and the couple didn't. He remembered the pinched, almost scared expression on Matthew's face. His daughter, Kim, used to be a great one for making up stories, but her face never looked like that when she was romancing. However, Kim had nothing to do with Matthew. He shrugged: coppers should deal in verifiable facts, not vague suppositions.

He sat down at his desk and flicked through the Jersey telephone directory. He might as well see this thing through. There were no Pilsen-Smiths. Assuming they had a phone, that meant they were either new arrivals on the island or ex-directory. The surname seemed vaguely familiar.

Peggy had a list of ex-directory numbers. Crozier emerged from his office with some typing for Peggy as Bergerac was leafing through it. Crozier gave him a sour look; Bergerac smiled cheerfully back.

The number was there. Bergerac made a note of it and retreated before Crozier could think of an excuse to keep him.

The phone rang three times before it was picked up.

'Old Highcliff Farm.'

'This is Detective Sergeant Bergerac of the Bureau des Etrangers. Who am I speaking to, please?'

'Mrs Jarrell. I'm the housekeeper.'

The voice was abrupt and Scottish.

'I wonder if you can help me. A small boy named Matthew dropped a key-ring in the Bureau earlier this morning. I'd like to return it to him.'

'There are no small boys here, Sergeant. And no one called Matthew.'

Bergerac persevered. 'His parents were with him. They drove off in a red Rover. I traced the number and – '

'Are you sure you got the number correctly?' She sounded exactly like a Glaswegian teacher who had terrorized Bergerac at his primary school. 'I believe we have a red Rover but I can assure you that there are no small boys in this house, with or without their parents. And now, if you'll excuse me, I have work to do.'

Mrs Jarrell put the phone down. Bergerac stared at the handset for a moment and swore softly under his breath. OK, so he might have made a mistake. There were plenty of red Rovers on the island.

There was nothing more he could do. Perhaps Matthew would discover his loss and pick up the key-ring from reception. It really didn't matter.

As he replaced the handset, the phone began to ring.

It was Crozier on the internal line.

'What's this I hear from Goddard?' he demanded. 'Wasting time on that kid's key-ring! I've got news for you, Jim: the Bureau isn't some kind of Lost Property Office. Understood?'

Diamanté Lil ran her pencil down the last column of figures.

'Well, that's all right,' she said with relief. 'It balances perfectly.' She looked up with a smile. 'Bar receipts are up on last quarter.'

Jean-Luc nodded. 'It's the Hotel de Bretagne arrangement. You were right, Madame.'

Diamanté Lil knew she was right. But it was nice to hear someone else say so. Jean-Luc – who combined the duties of head-waiter with those of deputy manager – had been against the idea when she first mentioned it. Lil was worried by the sharp decline in off-season profits; so was Jean-Luc, who thought it inevitable.

But Lil had come to an arrangement with the Bretagne, a hotel which specialized in French tourists. For a trial six months she offered their guests concessionary rates. The bar profits had vindicated her decision completely. The arrangement also helped to create the impression among other potential patrons that Lil's Place was fashionable. There is nothing quite so depressing as a nearly empty nightclub.

Lil stood up and stretched. 'Thank God that's over for another three months.' She scooped the papers together and fed them into an envelope. 'I'll send them to the accountant tomorrow.' She looked at her watch. 'I suppose I'd better go and circulate.'

Jean-Luc coughed. 'There is one other matter. Alvaro Ferreira.'

'Oh, yes. Just a minute.'

Lil unlocked the lefthand filing cabinet behind her desk. She kept the staff records here. She pulled out Ferreira's and glanced at the contents.

'You think we should take him on permanently?'

'I think so, Madame – despite the time of the year. He's very good. The patrons like him, and so do the staff. And the extra custom from the Bretagne means we need another waiter.'

'Only one thing worries me . . .'

'The drinking?' Jean-Luc shrugged. 'He doesn't do it here and it doesn't affect his work.'

'It's not just that.' Lil hesitated. 'I wish I knew *why* he had those two binges. He looks so sad sometimes.'

'That is part of his charm for some of our lady patrons,' Jean-Luc said drily.

'All right. If you're happy with him, that's the main thing. We'll keep him on.'

Lil led the way down from the office. She was pleased to see that the nightclub was busy. The Bretagne crowd had been augmented by several office parties. She looked quickly round. The price of a successful nightclub was constant vigilance – you couldn't afford to let your standards slip.

No one was waiting to be served; no one was behaving offensively. On the other hand, the new crooner was less than satisfactory. He was onstage at present, trying to imitate Frank Sinatra, without much success. Lil listened to him for a few minutes and made a mental note not to renew his contract. The man was too amateurish.

The dance floor was thick with swaying couples. As Lil picked her way around them, she was hailed by a familiar voice.

She turned. 'Jim! How nice. And Susan, I haven't seen you for weeks.'

'Come and join us,' Bergerac said.

'Just for a moment.'

Susan pulled out the chair beside her. Lil sat down at their table.

Alvaro Ferreira was at her elbow within seconds. 'Madame?'

'Just a glass of Perrier, please.'

He bowed and smiled. 'With one ice cube and a twist of lemon, I think.'

When Ferreira had left, Bergerac said: 'He looks happier than he did the last time I saw him.'

'He's joining us permanently,' Lil said. 'Jean-Luc's just told him.' She craned round and stared towards the entrance. 'You haven't seen Charlie Hungerford, have you?'

'Not yet.' Bergerac grinned. 'You can't wait to have his advice on your investments?'

'Is that what he told you?' Lil giggled. 'It's more like the

57

other way round. He's toying with the idea of setting up an entertainments consortium. He's trying to get me to come in with him.'

'And will you?'

Lil shook her head. 'I prefer to keep Charlie and my money in separate compartments. But I'll have to be tactful. He brings in a lot of business, one way or another.'

'We're meeting him too.'

Bergerac and Susan described the difficulties they were having with Kim's party. Lil listened intently.

'You'll have to do a deal,' she said. 'It's the only way. Charlie won't give you something for nothing – it's as simple as that.'

'Did I hear my name being taken in vain?'

Hungerford was only a couple of yards away, with Ferreira close behind him. His eyes swept round the table. The smile left his face when he saw Susan.

'Charlie!' Lil leapt to her feet and kissed his cheek. 'Alvaro, bring a bottle of champagne for Deputy Hungerford. The Ayala, I think.' She patted Charlie's hand. 'It's on the house, of course.'

'Very civil of you, Lil.' Hungerford contrived to create the impression that such civility was only his due. He sat down, nodding to Susan. 'Ah – Miss Young, isn't it?'

They had met several times before. Susan, ignoring the calculated rudeness, held out her hand. Charlie shook it gingerly.

'*Such* a good idea about Kim's party, Charlie,' Lil said. 'And a disco's just what she needs. She's going to be quite a social asset.'

'Eh?' Hungerford said.

Bergerac blinked.

The champagne arrived while Lil was talking. Hungerford couldn't get a word in edgeways. By the time he had downed a glass and a half of Ayala, he had not only agreed to the disco at Susan's place; he had also allowed himself

58

to be convinced that it was more or less his idea in the first place.

Lil hinted that solid business advantages could derive, albeit indirectly, from the party. Kim would be invited to other parties as a result. She would get to know the right sort of young people. And Hungerford, as a matter of course, would get to know the right sort of parents.

Leaning forward to gaze admiringly into Hungerford's eyes, Lil congratulated him on letting Kim have the disco at Susan's. It would make Kim seem much more independent and grown-up to her guests — a more desirable acquaintance, in fact. By the same token, the absence of obvious adult supervision was an advantage. Bergerac and Susan would be unobtrusively keeping an eye on things, of course; so there was nothing to worry about.

Bergerac watched Lil and marvelled. With her talents, he could have made Chief Inspector by now.

Hungerford lapped it up. He even unbent sufficiently to pour Susan a second glass of champagne.

At that point Lil suggested that she and Charlie adjourned to her office.

'You'll excuse us, won't you,' she said with the ghost of a wink to Bergerac and Susan. 'Charlie's advising me about some investments.'

'Ay,' Hungerford said. 'That's right. Always glad to help a lady. No offence, Lil,' he added with a leer, 'but a woman needs a man's guidance in some things. Eh?'

He stumbled to his feet and followed her towards the stairs.

'Will Lil be all right with him?' Susan asked.

Bergerac laughed. 'Don't worry. Where women are concerned, Charlie's bark is worse than his bite.'

Susan grinned. 'Did you notice? He took the rest of the champagne with him.'

*

59

Bergerac and Susan stayed for another hour.

They spent much of the time dancing. The crooner had given way to a small jazz band. It was after midnight when they left.

'I wish we could have stayed longer,' Susan said as Bergerac helped her into her coat.

'We can if you want.'

Susan smothered a yawn. 'I'm working tomorrow. Having fun takes it out of you.'

She opened the door to the street. A gust of cold air whipped through the gap. The temperature had dropped and clouds blanketed most of the sky. They had been planning to walk home but the outside world was uninviting. Hungerford's Rolls was parked directly outside the entrance.

'Looks like we might be in for another storm,' Bergerac said. 'Let's ring for a taxi.'

There were footsteps behind them. He swung round.

'Maybe there's no need,' Bergerac whispered. He raised his voice. 'I've just remembered something I want to ask him.'

Hungerford was still in a good mood. He was struggling into his overcoat and humming to himself. Bergerac decided on an oblique approach.

'Charlie. Got a moment? I wondered if you'd come across a bloke called Pilsen-Smith?'

'Old Guy? Course I have. One of our newcomers – completely renovated Old Highcliff Farm. He'll be a real asset to the community, you mark my words. He owns a controlling share of Pilsen's, you know.'

'The builders?' Bergerac remembered the slogan that accompanied their advertisements: *Own Your Own Pilsen Home*.

Hungerford nodded. 'One of the biggest in the UK. And they'll be even bigger if they get the Colton New Town job.

60

I know they're tendering for it. Colton'll make Milton Keynes look like Little-Doddering-in-the-Wold.' Hungerford glanced slyly at Bergerac. 'As a matter of fact, we might ask Guy to join the Committee. We've a vacancy coming up.' He raised a hand in farewell. 'Must be off. Goodnight.'

Bergerac raised his eyebrows. 'Are you going to offer us a lift, Charlie? Or shall I book you for parking on a yellow line?'

CHAPTER
7

'A large Scotch,' the newcomer said. 'Bell's, if you've got it. With ice and water.'

'Certainly, sir.'

With a flick of his eyes Jean-Luc passed the order on to Jamie, one of his subordinates. Jean-Luc only fetched and carried for favoured patrons. This man, dressed in a rumpled suit and with his tie hanging askew, looked like one of the minor businessmen who thronged the conference centres of the big hotels.

Lil touched Jean-Luc's arm. 'Table twenty-seven needs some refills.'

It was the evening after her meeting with Hungerford. Lil's Place was even more crowded than before. Tonight the star attraction was a comedian dressed as Father Christmas.

Jean-Luc returned to the bar. He beckoned to Alvaro. 'Take over Jamie's order, will you – a large Bell's for the man by himself at table fifteen. Jamie, get over to twenty-seven.' He injected a carefully calculated touch of sternness into his voice: 'You should have had your eye on them.'

Jamie scuttled away. Alvaro reached for a whisky glass. Jean-Luc smiled to himself. He ran a tight ship here; it was the only way. If you let the waiters get slack, the service suffered; if the service suffered, the customers would eventually move on to another nightclub.

Lil took one last look around and climbed the stairs to her office. It might be busy, but at least none of the patrons tonight needed her personal touch. At times last night she had wondered if she would ever be able to get rid of that damned Charlie Hungerford. Still, the man was too important to offend. A friendly deputy was worth his weight in gold.

What she really wanted now was a cup of tea. Then she would lock herself into her office and put her feet up for ten minutes. Being the boss had its compensations.

She collected the cup and saucer from her desk and went along to the staff kitchen at the end of the corridor. It was a clean, well-lit room whose amenities ranged from a microwave oven to a small freezer. Lil believed in pampering her staff. The investment paid off in the end: you attracted the best on the market, and they tended to stay loyal. Next to the kitchen was a comfortable staff sitting room.

The kettle seemed to take hours to boil. Lil leant against the counter and rubbed her eyes. She caught sight of her face in the mirror over the sink. God, she looked old. Too many late nights.

There were hurried footsteps in the corridor, followed by the sound of the sitting-room door opening and closing. Lil looked at her watch and frowned. It was only 10.45. The staff were not due to begin their series of tea breaks until eleven. Someone was trying to pull a fast one.

The kettle boiled. Lil decided to make the tea before she investigated. Maybe the truant had a good excuse. She hoped so. Chivvying the staff was not an activity she relished.

Thirty seconds later she heard a dull clunk, which sent a tremor through the kitchen.

The fire-escape door?

Lil forgot her tea. She rushed into the corridor. The fire escape was next to the kitchen on the other side from the sitting room. The door was closed but the bar was not

63

completely in place. She pushed it open and felt for the light switch.

The iron fire escape was empty. So was the small yard at the back of the club. A thin drizzle was falling. She heard the sound of running footsteps, growing fainter every second.

Lil swore. Another sneak thief? They'd had the same problem last July – someone had rifled the lockers in the sitting room. But surely the thief wouldn't have had time to nick much? He could only have been in the room for a few seconds.

She ducked back into the corridor and charged into the sitting room. The light was on. All but one of the lockers were still closed. Lil glanced at the name tag on the door.

Alvaro Ferreira.

The locker itself was empty.

'They are in good health. Considering everything.'

It was a woman's voice this time. The line was bad and Danston wondered how far away she was. The phone was a horrible medium of communication. He clung to the thought – it was one of those safe generalizations that couldn't hurt you.

His mind worried the notion like a dog worries a bone, nibbling away the illusion of safety. Phones disembodied the people who used them. It reduced them to ghosts. Ghosts were dead. Dead people didn't speak. Emma wasn't talking. Emma was dead . . .

The knuckles of the hand that grasped the telephone had turned white. *The bones are coming through the skin.* No, he mustn't allow himself to be subjective; that road led to madness. Danston tried to be objective about the phenomenon: *I must be under stress.*

'Are you there?' the woman said.

A good question, Danston thought. He said: 'I want Emma. I . . . I *need* her, you see.'

'You must be working very hard at present,' the voice went on. 'The Colton New Town contract. It's good to keep busy, isn't it? That's why Emma went away. She'll be back when you've finished, just as long as you do as you're told.'

'Oh, I will,' Danston said. 'But when will Emma – '

'We'll discuss the arrangements later. Goodnight.'

The ghost went away. John Danston stared at the handset. Without the voice, it was just a piece of plastic enclosing a few wires – as useless as a body without a mind and soul. As useless as he was without Emma.

Diamanté Lil had turned down the offer of a chair and was standing by the Christmas tree.

The desk sergeant tried to make conversation. He liked the look of her. Give him a mature woman, any day – someone who knew what was what. And this one was more than a good looker: she had a touch of sparkle too. He sniffed her perfume appreciatively.

But Lil answered him in monosyllables. She was examining the Christmas tree as if she had never seen one before. The sergeant had decorated it himself, so he was inclined to rate her interest in it as another point in her favour.

He tried again. 'Shame there aren't any presents on it. The Chief Inspector wasn't feeling too generous this year.'

She looked blankly at him.

'Joke,' he explained.

'Oh, yes,' she said absently. 'Of course.'

Bergerac walked into the reception area. Lil looked up, a smile lighting her face.

Bloody plainclothes, the desk sergeant thought. They have all the luck.

*

'I hope I'm not wasting your time.' Lil frowned and fiddled with the clasp of her handbag. 'I was just passing the Bureau, you see, and I thought I'd pop in. On the off-chance you were here. I wanted a word – well, unofficially, I suppose.'

'Spit it out,' Bergerac said with a grin. Lil's hesitation was uncharacteristic. He tried to prompt her. 'Something may be wrong but you're not quite sure?'

'Yes.' The frown vanished for a moment. 'It's my womanly intuition, Jim. I know you policemen think it's a weakness.'

'Try me.'

'You remember that Portuguese waiter? The one who got drunk? I think he served you the night before last.'

Bergerac nodded. 'Alvaro Ferreira.'

'That's the one. He seems to have vanished.'

'You reckon he's on another bender?'

'I don't know. He went home early last night and it was rather odd, and this morning I – '

'Hang on, Lil – you've lost me. You saw him last night and he was on duty?'

She nodded. 'He was meant to be on all night. But he had some sort of fainting fit at about a quarter to eleven. Jean-Luc told me – I was upstairs. He came round almost at once, but he obviously wasn't well. Jean-Luc wanted to send him home. Even called him a taxi.'

'You look after your staff all right,' Bergerac said.

Lil shrugged. 'We try. But in this case we didn't succeed. Alvaro went upstairs to get his coat – said he was perfectly OK by himself. I was in the staff kitchen, and I heard him. He emptied his locker and went down the fire escape.'

'So? Maybe he felt the fresh air would do him good.'

'Yes – that's exactly what he said.'

'You mean you saw him *again* last night?'

Lil gave him a rueful smile. 'I'm telling this the wrong

way, aren't I? After he'd gone I left it twenty minutes and phoned him at home. He was fine – apologized for not taking the taxi; said he had this desperate need for air. Told me he'd be in tomorrow – today, I mean. But he's not. And there's something else. When he left last night he emptied his locker.'

Bergerac blinked. 'So you said.'

'But I mean *really* emptied it. Not just his outdoor things.'

'What else was there?'

'All the waiters keep a spare shirt and trousers in their lockers. And shoe polish – stuff like that. Jean-Luc's a stickler for smartness. There are always spillages when you're serving food and drink.'

'Any reason why he should do a bunk?'

'Just the opposite. We'd just told him he'd passed his probation. He was over the moon about it.'

'And he hadn't been drinking?'

'No way. Jean-Luc or I would have known.'

'But when you phoned him, he said he was coming into work today.'

'Maybe he couldn't face telling me he was leaving. Not directly.'

'How did he sound on the phone? Like he usually did?'

Lil sighed. 'I don't know. I'd never talked to him on the phone before. People always sound different.' She paused. 'I thought he seemed tired, perhaps a bit breathless.' She added with devastating frankness: 'But I might have imagined that. I was *expecting* him to sound off-colour.'

Bergerac grinned. 'You'd make a great witness. Where does he live?'

'Oxford Road – near the gas-works. I drove over there on my way here. He rents a room at a sort of boarding-house called Carlton House. The name's misleading – it's pretty sleazy.'

'I presume he wasn't there. Did you speak to the landlady or the manager?'

Lil shivered. 'There was an old woman – she opened the door. She hadn't seen him since yesterday.'

Bergerac had noticed the shiver. 'You didn't take to her?'

'She wasn't exactly helpful,' Lil admitted. 'Jim, what do you think I should do? Can you help?'

'I think he'll turn up in an hour or two,' Bergerac said. 'He's got a weakness for booze. So the odds are he's gone on a binge. Probably sleeping it off somewhere.'

'But he wouldn't have let us down like that. He – '

'You can't know what a drunk's going to do,' Bergerac interrupted. His voice hardened. 'Believe me, I know. All too well.'

'Jim, love, you're through all that.'

Bergerac shook his head. He hated being on the receiving end of sympathy, even when the giver was someone he liked as much as Lil. Furthermore, she was wrong: he wasn't through it. He had learned long ago that ruthless self-honesty was the only way to deal with this.

'No one's ever through it,' he said slowly. 'The point is, I know how drunks behave. Don't expect them to act rationally. And the only consistent thing about their behaviour is the fact that they drink.'

Lil screwed up her face. 'It's just that Alvaro wouldn't go off without telling me. He's not like that.'

'Womanly intuition again?' Bergerac shrugged. 'Look, as a friend, I'd say you shouldn't worry because he's probably on a drinking spree. As a copper I can't do anything unless you formally report him as a missing person – which could be embarrassing for all concerned if he turns up in an hour or two with a God-awful hangover again.'

There was a moment's silence. The door behind Lil opened and Crozier came into the office. Crozier looked coldly at Bergerac.

68

'OK,' Lil said. 'I'm reporting him as a missing person. Where do we go from here?'

'We find a form and fill it in,' Bergerac said. 'I spend half my working life filling in forms.'

'Missing person?' Crozier said. 'Hullo, Lil. Who?'

'One of Lil's waiters.'

'Immigrant?'

Bergerac nodded. 'Portuguese.'

'Ah, well,' Crozier said, as if Ferreira's nationality explained everything. 'What can you expect? Probably slipped off home for Christmas.'

CHAPTER
8

'Not seafood,' Norma Jean Veldman said. 'I've gone off seafood for life.'

Ronny Quine studied the menu. 'I'm having steak.'

'You always do,' Norma said. 'With chips. And you like Heinz tomato sauce with it. That's one of the things that make you stand out in a crowd. You're so bloody predictable.'

'Look, Norma – '

'I'll have the chicken,' she informed the barman.

She picked up her gin and tonic and left Quine to pay. They were in a bar overlooking St Aubin's harbour. She sat down at a vacant table and stared with loathing at the view, which was partially obscured by the fishing nets that did duty as curtains. After that trip across the Channel the other night, she was finished with the sea. All that bloody water – heaving and tossing and swaying. She had never felt so ill in her life. When they left this God-forsaken island, she was going home by plane – and damn the risk.

Quine rejoined her. He had taken advantage of her absence to freshen his glass.

'That's your third double in half an hour,' she said peevishly. 'What *are* you trying to do? Turn yourself into a lush?'

'Things are going well,' Quine said. 'We deserve a little celebration. Danston's cooperating nicely. There's no trouble this end – '

'No trouble?' Norma Jean pursed her mouth. 'Are you

that stupid? The Danston business is a side issue, whatever Oliver thinks.'

'It's a nice little money-spinner.'

'It's peanuts compared with the other thing.' She lit a menthol cigarette and blew the smoke across the table. 'You blew it last night. Don't you realize?'

'Just a temporary hitch,' Quine said. 'On an island this size he can't go far.'

The smugness in his voice infuriated her. Ronny had his uses, but he needed to be kept in his place. Like so many men, he assumed that if you let him into your bed you were willing to let him control your life.

Norma scowled at him. 'What makes you think he's still on Jersey? He could be back on the mainland. Or he might be in France by now. That hydrofoil to St Malo only takes about – '

'He's here,' Quine said. 'Take it from me, love – he'll be too scared to leave. He's not a pro.'

She switched the line of her attack: 'It beats me how you could let him recognize you.'

'I didn't recognize him – that was the problem. Not right away. He's shaved off his beard. It was only when he brought my drink that the penny dropped. And by that time he'd had a good look at me.'

'Well, you'd better find him. Quickly.'

'Norma, love – be reasonable.' He stretched his hand under the table and squeezed her knee. 'What's the hurry?'

She brushed Quine's hand away. 'Use your head. We're not the only ones who're looking for him.'

He frowned. 'But who else knows? When Yellowthorn died – '

The expression on Norma Jean's face stopped him in mid-sentence.

'The police, Ronny,' she said gently. 'You remember?

Your ex-colleagues. We gave them the best of reasons to look for him.'

Quine gulped down the rest of his whisky. His face was flushed.

'OK, darling,' he said. 'You've got a point. But *we* aren't responsible for that. *You* are. And don't tell me the knife slipped, because I won't believe you.'

Norma Jean's eyes were blank – as though she were looking at something inside her mind. What she saw there must have pleased her, for she smiled.

Quine said hurriedly: 'I'll go back to Lil's Place tonight. If he's there, I'll get him on his way home. It shouldn't take long to make him talk. And afterwards you can do whatever you want.'

'But what if he isn't there?' she asked.

He shrugged. 'I start pub-crawling, I suppose. He'll go where the booze is.'

'There might be a quicker way.'

'Like what?'

'If we just find out where he lives.'

'I'm looking for Alvaro Ferreira,' Bergerac said. 'I understand he lives here.'

'You what?'

Bergerac repeated what he'd said in a much louder voice.

'All right,' the old woman snarled, 'you needn't shout. I'm not deaf. He's not in.'

The door closed with a bang. Bergerac looked ruefully at it for a few seconds. It had stained glass in the upper section. Though the paint was chipped and cracked, the woodwork itself was solid enough. The Victorians knew how to build.

He stepped back from the little porch. On either side of the door was a bay window. Carlton House was one of those comfortable little villas that had mushroomed out from the old centre of St Helier in the nineteenth century. It had somehow escaped the post-war vogue for redevelopment and renovation; perhaps the old woman was a sitting tenant on a long lease. The house was long overdue for repairs. The stucco was crumbling. Leaking gutters had stained the outside walls. There was an ominous crack in one of the chimney stacks. The tiny front garden was crammed with battered dustbins.

A net curtain twitched in the window on his right. Bergerac rapped on the glass. The landlady pulled aside the curtain. Her mouth moved, saying the same words over and over again. You didn't have to be an expert lip-reader to know what they were.

Bergerac pulled out his wallet. He laid his warrant card against the glass and pointed at the door.

Her face remained ferocious; but now there was also a touch of fear in her expression. The yellowing curtain fell back into position. Footsteps shuffled down the hall. Bergerac braced himself. The door opened. Stale air wafted out, mingling the smell of old food and old dirt with a faint odour of something that was even less savoury. Defective drains?

As before, she kept the door on the chain.

'Mrs Le Davre?'

She nodded.

'I'm from the Bureau des Etrangers. Detective Sergeant Bergerac. May I come in?'

Mrs Le Davre looked blankly at him.

'We're looking for Mr Ferreira,' Bergerac said. 'He *is* one of your lodgers, isn't he?'

'I told you,' she said. 'He's not in. You deaf or something?'

'His employer has reported him missing. I'd like to ask you a few questions and have a look at his room.'

'Haven't got time,' she snapped. 'You young blokes are worse than the bloody Gestapo.'

'It won't take long, Mrs Le Davre.'

'Well, you can't.' A note of triumph crept into her voice. 'You haven't got a search warrant, have you? So you can't come in.'

The door began to close.

Bergerac was tempted to remind her that the Gestapo hadn't bothered with legal trifles like search warrants. Instead he said: 'When was your last Public Health inspection, Mrs Le Davre?'

The door stopped moving.

'What's that to you?'

'Nothing.' Bergerac smiled. 'As I told you, I'm from the Bureau. Of course we do liaise with the Public Health Department. When and if we think it's necessary.'

There was a long silence. Mrs Le Davre's grubby hand tightened on the door jamb. She wore an antiquated pink housecoat. A strand of greasy hair trailed across her left cheek. She was an unpleasant old woman, but she was also very vulnerable. Bergerac was ashamed of himself.

'I don't think we need trouble the Public Health Department,' Bergerac said. 'Do you?'

Her shoulders twitched in what might have been a shrug. She unhooked the chain from the door and stood back to allow him to enter.

The smell was much worse in the hall. The smell of poverty was not something that people associated with Jersey, but Bergerac was familiar with it. Most policemen were.

A dusty cheese plant wilted on the hall table. Around it were piles of uncollected letters – bills and circulars, by the look of them; the sort of mail no one wanted to open. Bergerac skimmed through the envelopes. None of them was addressed to Ferreira.

74

Mrs Le Davre slipped past him, the heels of her slippers slapping against the cracked linoleum. At the foot of the stairs she paused.

'I thought you said you wanted to see his room.'

'I do. But I'd like to ask you a few questions first.'

'If you must.' She pulled out a packet of cigarettes from the pocket of her housecoat. She squinted up at him as she lit the cigarette. 'What you waiting for, then?'

'When did you last see Mr Ferreira?'

'I don't know. Yesterday, was it?'

'You tell me.'

'All right, yesterday. I give him his breakfast round eight-thirty. I know he works nights, but I said to him, "You can't expect me to change my routine just for you. I do breakfast between seven-thirty and nine, and if you're not there, that's your hard luck." So sometimes he came down and sometimes he didn't. Not that it made any difference to what he paid me, mind; bed-and-breakfast, that's what I do, and that's what they pay me for. There's nothing wrong with that and — '

'I'm sure it's all above board, Mrs Le Davre,' Bergerac interrupted. 'Do you know what he did after breakfast?'

'I suppose he went out.'

'What about his room?'

'Well, I don't know.' Mrs Le Davre glanced at him; a defensive note entered her voice. 'Some of my regulars like to look after their own rooms. And why shouldn't they? I value my privacy myself, so I know how they feel. What's it to me if they want to make their own beds?'

Less work, for a start. It was becoming increasingly clear that Mrs Le Davre kept her lodgers strictly in line: they were a means of earning the maximum profit for the minimum effort.

'Did he spend much time here?' Bergerac asked.

She shook her head.

'Did you check up on him when he didn't come down for breakfast this morning?'

'No, of course I didn't. I told you: sometimes he didn't come down. If you come to that, some nights he didn't come home at all.'

'How often?'

'Once or twice.'

That made sense, Bergerac thought: Ferreira's benders tended to be all-night affairs.

'If you ask me,' Mrs Le Davre went on, 'he had a woman somewhere. There was this woman come round this morning. Tarted up like a dog's breakfast, she was. She wanted to know where he was.' She sniffed. 'I don't allow that sort of thing here. It's not right. If my lodgers want to behave like animals, they can do it somewhere else. I don't want their fancy women on the doorstep. I sent her off with a flea in her ear. The cheek of it!'

Bergerac smothered a grin, wondering how Lil had reacted to this slur on her character. In all probability she hadn't had time to get a word in edgeways before the door was slammed in her face.

Mrs Le Davre glanced at him again, presumably to check that he'd registered this virtuous statement in her favour. A cylinder of ash fell from her cigarette, disintegrated on the housecoat and showered on to the linoleum. She brushed the side of her housecoat.

'Did you hear him come in last night?'

'No – why should I?'

'He had his own key?'

She nodded. 'I give my regulars a key to the side door. They pay a deposit, of course. I used not to charge but so many keys were lost I had to do something.'

'There's a phone here?'

Mrs Le Davre pointed upwards. 'On the second floor. A pay phone.'

76

'Did it ring last night?'

'I don't know, do I?' She looked at him, exasperation overlaying the fear on her face. 'I live on the ground floor. Besides, I had the telly on.'

And she was hard of hearing as well. Mrs Le Davre could hardly have been a worse witness if she tried. Perhaps she was trying.

Bergerac followed her up the stairs. She took him up to the second landing. Wheezing, she fumbled for a bunch of keys in the pocket of her housecoat. All the bedrooms had Yale locks and numbers on their doors. The bathroom door was open, revealing a geyser that might have been new when Edward VII was on the throne.

'What's he like about money?' Bergerac asked.

'He's paid up to the end of the month.' Mrs Le Davre tried one key in the lock of Number 12. She swore when it refused to turn. 'Give him his due, he's always been regular. Not like some I could name.'

The next key fitted. She pushed the door open, revealing a long, narrow room with a sloping ceiling. It was about six feet wide and fifteen feet long – almost certainly partitioned off from the room next door. The door was in one of the shorter walls; opposite it was a window which overlooked Oxford Road.

The air was fresher here: the top of the sash window was slightly open. The room was sparsely furnished, with a single bed, neatly covered with a purple and much stained candlewick bedspread, a small wardrobe, an armchair and a table. A small electric fire stood on the orange carpet.

Mrs Le Davre crossed the room and closed the window with a bang. 'No wonder it's cold in here,' she said. 'These foreigners just don't think, do they?'

The room depressed Bergerac even more than the rest of the house had done. It was ugly and impersonal – and it was Ferreira's home. There were few obvious signs of

77

occupation beyond the fact that everything was clean and tidy. A dozen magazines were piled by the bed. A cheap transistor radio shared the table with an alarm clock, an ashtray, a mug and an electric kettle.

'Mind if I look round?' Bergerac said.

'Suit yourself.'

Mrs Le Davre leant against the wall. Bergerac moved in a clockwise direction round the room. There was nothing under the mattress or tucked among the magazines. The magazines themselves were mainly old colour supplements from the Sunday newspapers, together with a handful of travel brochures. The mug was clean and the transistor was tuned to Radio 2. A Marlboro had been stubbed out in the ashtray. There were no pictures, but a small crucifix hung above the head of the bed.

He turned his attention to the wardrobe. On top of it was a cheap blue suitcase which proved to be empty. The lock was broken. Inside the wardrobe he found a large tin which functioned as Ferreira's larder. Apart from sugar, instant coffee and powdered milk, he appeared to live solely on mouldy cheese and Ritz biscuits.

Two pairs of black trousers and three white shirts hung on the rail. Stacked beside them on shelves were the rest of Ferreira's clothes. On the bottom shelf was a carrier bag full of dirty washing.

Bergerac turned to Mrs Le Davre. 'These are mainly work clothes. What else did he wear?'

'In the day?' She scratched her head. 'I think he had some jeans. He had one of those fisherman's sweaters, I'm sure of that – I remember him buying it. And he had a sort of car coat he wore outside – bit like a donkey jacket.'

Bergerac stooped and ran his hand underneath the wardrobe. The tips of his fingers brushed against a box which had been tucked to one side. He pulled it out.

It was a shoebox. There were a few papers inside –

leaflets from the Immigration and Nationality Department, a map of St Helier and a list of registered guesthouses. Bergerac wondered what else the box had contained. A passport and work permit? Money?

'Don't forget the waste-paper basket,' Mrs Le Davre said with the hint of a sneer. 'I know you coppers like to be thorough.'

The basket was concealed behind the open door. Ferreira had lined it with a plastic bag. There were more cigarette butts, an empty crisp packet and a framed picture.

Or rather – a frame without a picture.

Bergerac frowned. He picked up the frame and gently blew the ash away from it. It was a simple, white plastic affair with a hardboard back. The glass was intact.

'What's this doing here?' he asked.

'Don't ask me,' Mrs Le Davre said. 'It's not mine. It used to hang over there.'

She pointed to a nail on the wall above the table.

Bergerac tapped the glass with a fingernail. 'Why should he throw it away?'

'Search me. You're the detective.'

'What was the picture of?'

'A woman, I think.' Mrs Le Davre hesitated, looking slyly at him. 'Black hair, maybe, sort of foreign looking.'

There was no 'maybe' about it. Bergerac was prepared to bet that Mrs Le Davre snooped in her lodgers' rooms while they were out. It was feasible that she'd known about the shoebox – which opened up some interesting possibilities.

Bergerac filed the thought away for the future. 'A photo, was it?'

She gave a decisive shake of her head. 'A painting.'

'What sort of painting? The kind you buy in Woolworth's?'

'No.' Mrs Le Davre hesitated. 'It looked like a real person. Know what I mean?'

He turned the frame over and shook out the hardboard backing. Inside he found a small label:

PYGMALION PORTRAITURE
Your Loved Ones – Our Works of Art
Ref. No. 88/326/BJ

Underneath was a London telephone number.

'Mind if I take this?' Bergerac said. 'I'll give you a receipt.'

'If you want.' She paused, biting her lip. 'What's all this about? Is he coming back?'

Bergerac shrugged. 'If I knew that, Mrs Le Davre, I wouldn't be here.'

CHAPTER
9

Detective Chief Inspector Barney Crozier prided himself on his memory.

Memory, he was accustomed to say in the first of the introductory lectures he gave to each new batch of recruits, was the backbone of detection. In the final analysis, it was more important than the most sophisticated technology, the most penetrating powers of deduction, the luckiest hunches or the most painstaking assemblage of evidence. Memory, whether fully conscious or not, allowed you to make connections between people, events and crimes. It was like the operating system that allowed you to use a variety of programs on the same computer. Technology, deduction, intuition and evidence needed memory to function properly, just as – ahd Crozier was never afraid to mix his metaphors – a car needed petrol.

He urged recruits to train their memories; it was, he said, the vital Faculty X of police work. In the discussions that followed the lectures, Crozier was often asked to illustrate the use of memory from his own experiences, and to recommend techniques of memorizing.

Consequently, it was particularly galling whenever Crozier's memory failed to operate at its usual pitch of efficiency. The failure attacked him on both a personal and a professional level.

On this occasion the lapse occurred early in the afternoon. He had had a working lunch with the officer in charge of the St Brelade police station in St Aubin. After an unsatisfactory discussion about the arrests quota, Crozier left; he was not in a good mood even at this juncture. His car was parked behind the police station. As he was unlocking the door he happened to glance across the road.

A man was studying the window of a newsagent's shop. He paused to grind out a cigarette with the heel of his shoe on the pavement. Crozier started his engine and edged the car towards the road. The man turned for a second. Crozier glimpsed heavy shoulders, made broader by a bulky leather jacket, a square, tanned face with a broken nose and short, curly grey hair.

Crozier's memory twitched. But the twitch was unproductive.

The man went into the shop. Crozier found a gap in the traffic, turned right and drove along the A1 to St Helier. During the short journey he prodded his memory mercilessly, trying to force it to explain why that face had seemed familiar. His mood worsened as his memory failed to cooperate.

Somewhere, he knew, he had seen that man before. It might have been anywhere – in the street, in a restaurant, perhaps. He might well be one of Jersey's residents; the island had a population of only 75,000, and you were constantly running into people whose faces you knew.

It didn't matter who the bloke was: the only thing that mattered was that Barney Crozier's memory had failed to come up with the goods on him.

At the Bureau there were two urgent messages from Charlie Hungerford. Hungerford's messages were always urgent. Crozier snapped at Peggy, who took it philosophically, as usual, and retired to his office. He hardly had time to sit down before the phone rang.

'Hello, Barney? Charlie Hungerford here. Glad I caught you at last. Now, I've been thinking. About the arrests quota.'

82

'Oh, God,' Crozier muttered.

'What was that?'

'Just clearing my throat.'

'Well, as I was saying,' Hungerford rushed on, 'maybe we should set up a coordinating sub-committee to monitor progress. Say five people – two policemen, two people from the Law and Order Committee and me in the chair. What do you think?'

What Crozier thought was unprintable.

Policemen weren't supposed to follow unsupported hunches – especially other people's.

But it was difficult to deny Diamanté Lil when she had set her heart on something. She never wheedled; she never presumed on old friendship or past favours; but somehow you found yourself doing exactly as she wanted.

After lunch, Bergerac sat down at his desk and dialled the London number. He recognized the exchange: south of the river, definitely; maybe somewhere like Catford. He had realized long ago that a reasonable working knowledge of London was an advantage even to a Jersey-based police-man. The capital exported crime to the island, along with wealthy tax-exiles, big banks and offshore trusts.

'Pygmalion Portraiture. Good afternoon. How can I help you?'

The woman who answered the phone reeled off the words as though she were a computerized voice-chip with a public-school education. Still, the intention at least was polite.

'This is Detective Sergeant Bergerac of the Jersey States Police. Can I speak to the manager, please?'

There was a muffled squawk at the other end of the line. 'Who did you say you were?' The voice had suddenly become human.

Bergerac repeated what he had said. 'Jersey,' he added

drily. 'You know, that island in the Channel where England blends with France.'

The young woman giggled. 'I know. I went there last summer. Super beaches. I – '

Bergerac cut into her holiday reminiscences: 'Is the manager available?'

'Well, actually, I'm the manager. As well as being the Girl Friday, secretary, tea lady and sole proprietor. By the way, I'm Elizabeth Enfield. Do you want to place an order?'

'*Your Loved Ones – Our Works of Art?*' Bergerac quoted. 'What exactly do you do?'

'I paint portraits from photos at twenty-five quid a go. That's one face, of course – extra faces in the same painting are fifteen quid each. I know it seems a lot, but faces are the difficult bit, you see. Watercolour, of course. Ten inches by eight is my standard size – I never liked large-scale work. I'll do it, of course, if the customer wants it, but it comes expensive. Frames extra, I'm afraid, but we really have a lovely selection. And – '

'Ms Enfield, I really – '

'Call me Liz, Sergeant – everyone else does. I don't suppose I can immortalize your old Granny, can I? Or capture little Sebastian's first smile for posterity? We do a mail-order service, you know. Distance no object. Only a small fee towards postage and packing.'

She sounded very young and very enthusiastic.

'Not this time,' Bergerac said. 'I'm trying to trace the location of a man who had one of your pictures. Presumably one of your customers. Perhaps you could check your records for me?'

'Do you have the reference number?'

'*88/326/BJ,*' Bergerac read out.

'Police enlist the aid of amateur sleuth,' Liz muttered at the other end; the line was good, and he could hear a rustling as if she was flicking through a file or a card-index. 'Dauntless girl-artist astonishes Scotland Yard . . . Here we are. October this year. Ordered on the third and collected on the eighteenth. Bloke named Bernardo Jacinto.'

'You sure about that? The name, I mean?'

'Quite sure – it's on the card. Actually, I remember him fairly well. He was one of my first customers. I only started in September, after I finished at Art College.' She ignored Bergerac's attempt to stem the flow. 'My friends say I'm prostituting my profession, but you've got to earn a living, haven't you? And Renoir painted from photos, so I don't see why I shouldn't. Anyway, most of them are still on the dole, my friends, I mean; so if I am selling out, it's worth it. I'd rather be a small business person than one of the unemployment statistics. What do you think?'

'I agree with Renoir,' Bergerac said. 'Can you describe Jacinto?'

'Well – sort of small and swarthy, I suppose. Oh, and he had a beard – one of those little pointy ones like Napoleon III used to have.'

'An imperial?'

'That's it. I imagined he was Spanish or South American. Definitely the Latin type. Had rather a nice smile. Very gentle.'

The description fitted, Bergerac thought, apart from the beard. There again it fitted a lot of other people too. But if it had been Alvaro Ferreira, why bother with a false name?

'Who did he want painted?' Bergerac asked. 'A woman?'

'But you've got the painting,' Liz said.

'No, we haven't. Just the frame with your label on it.'

'It was a woman – his wife, he said. He wanted the painting as a surprise for her birthday.'

'What did she look like? Can you remember?'

'I can do better than that – I take a Polaroid of everything I do. Here we are: just an ordinary middle-aged woman with dark hair and a narrow face. I can't see much of her dress – it looks like a black sack. She's sitting by a table outside; there's a striped awning – it could be in a café.'

Bergerac made a note on his pad. 'Did you get an address for him?'

'No, I don't think so.' There was a pause on the other end of the line. 'That's right, he paid cash in advance and said he'd call back in a fortnight. No point in getting an address.'

'Sounds a trusting sort of bloke,' Bergerac said. 'Well, thanks very much, er – Liz.'

'Is that all?' She squeaked with mock-outrage; the squeak dissolved into another giggle. 'Don't you want to ask some more questions?'

'Not just at present, thanks.'

'Don't you even want a copy of the Polaroid? Or the artist's opinion of the suspect? You know, the trained intuition of one who has painted the souls behind a hundred faces?'

'All right,' Bergerac said. 'What was he like? Would you buy a used car from him?'

There was a moment's silence.

'Probably,' Liz said slowly. 'He was such a nice little man. And a bit sad with it. Aroused my dormant maternal instincts, which is another way of saying that I found him a teensy-weensy bit sexy. Does that sound stupid to you?'

Bergerac remembered Lil's opinion of Ferreira – and how the waiter was reputed to affect some of her female patrons. 'No – it ties in with what other people have said.'

'And so gentle with it. I tell you one thing, Sergeant: he wouldn't hurt a fly, I'm sure of that.'

*

86

The files had disgorged their contents over the sitting-room carpet. He felt as though he was drowning in a sea of paper. On one wall he had thumbtacked the Technical Services' plan of the site. Fields. A few cottages. A gently winding river. A belt of trees. He remembered Emma saying that it was a pity they couldn't find somewhere less pretty to desecrate.

Emma – he mustn't think about her. There was work to do. He was already behind the schedule he had set himself.

Thank God for the work, Danston thought. The comforting and familiar routine of assessing tenders filled his mind. He could cope with it. It was good to know there was something he could cope with. He picked up his biro and scored a line in the margin of Paragraph 3.04.2 in the Pilsen proposal. In view of the lie of the land, they would have problems with the shopping mall's drainage. You'd have thought they would have taken something as obvious as that into account.

The door chimes rang, snapping his concentration.

Danston stood up automatically. The papers on his lap cascaded to the floor. Then for an instant the panic threatened to choke him. A visitor? He didn't want visitors. The voices on the phone had warned him about visitors. They might put Emma in danger.

The chimes rang again.

He still hadn't shaved – he must look strange. On the other hand, the car was outside so the visitor must know he was in. It would look stranger if he didn't answer the door. It might be the postman or even the rector. Please God, not the rector.

Danston dashed into the hall, shutting the door on the chaos in the sitting room. The blurred outline of a man was visible through the frosted glass of the front door. The chimes rang out for the third time. Danston took a deep breath and opened the door.

'Hello, John, old son,' George Littledean said. 'How's it going?'

The councillor took a step forward so there was barely twelve inches between their faces. His body was wrapped in a sheepskin coat which increased his resemblance to a bear.

'Fine,' Danston stammered. 'Everything's fine.'

'Turned parky, hasn't it? I don't wonder you're at home. Best place to be.'

'I'm working, Mr Littledean,' Danston said.

'I know – Ned Arlen told me. Very wise. I hear you got the house to yourself.'

Danston nodded. 'Emma's away – '

'So there's nothing to disturb you?' Littledean gave a throaty chuckle. 'Except me. Just happened to be passing, John. Thought I'd pop in and see how the Colton job's going. The Committee meeting's not that far away. Of course if there's anything you want to discuss, unofficial like, I'd be only too glad to help.'

'No, no, there's not.'

'Everything under control then? That's what I like to hear.' Littledean's eyes flickered past Danston, as if he was debating the possibility of barging into the house to see for himself. 'Some of my Committee members were a little bit worried – thought we were overloading you, perhaps. It's a big responsibility.'

'I'm coping, thank you.' Danston made an immense effort to look Littledean in the eyes. 'Now, if you'll excuse me – '

'Of course. I know you're busy.'

Littledean half turned, raising a hand in farewell. Suddenly he paused; Danston's relief vanished.

'Just one thing, John. Don't think I'm trying to hurry you. But have you got a front-runner out of those tenders?'

Danston swallowed. 'It's early days yet, Mr Littledean,' he heard himself saying. 'But Pilsen's look good.'

CHAPTER
10

'What is all this?' Bergerac said. 'A conspiracy or something?'

Diamanté Lil grinned at him. 'A conspiracy to buy you a drink. What are you having?'

Bergerac gave in and ordered a tonic water. He had arranged to meet Susan at Odell's, a small wine bar which had recently opened in Halkett Place. Lil had somehow managed to join the party.

It was still early in the evening. Both he and Susan had come straight from work. Odell's was nearly empty.

Bergerac intercepted a glance between the two women. 'What's it all about?' he asked suspiciously. 'Kim's party?'

Susan shook her head. 'No problems there – thanks to Lil.'

'That's why I phoned Susan,' Lil said. 'We've got some glasses you can use – odds and ends we brought from the Royal Barge: it doesn't matter if they all get broken. And the other thing is, you can order the drinks through us. At trade prices – it's quite a saving.'

'Thanks,' Bergerac said. 'Somehow I've got this feeling that there's more to come.'

'Well, Susan mentioned you were meeting here, and asked if I would like to come along. And I said, "Yes, please" – I haven't been here before and I like to investigate the competition.'

'You haven't got a wine bar,' Bergerac pointed out. 'Remember?'

'Not yet. But I'm always interested in new opportunities. Like your ex-father-in-law.'

'We were wondering,' Susan said, 'if you had any news about Alvaro?'

'Ah, so that's it. Don't say you think he's sexy too?'

'Well, he is rather sweet. It's that Little-Boy-Lost look of his.'

Bergerac told them briefly the results of his investigation so far. They did not add up to much. Ferreira seemed to have left his room in Carlton House of his own free will. Barry Goddard had spent most of the afternoon checking the ferries and the airport; he had found nothing to suggest that Ferreira had left the island, though the possibility could not be ruled out. The empty frame in Ferreira's waste-paper basket had led to Pygmalion Portraiture in the Catford area of London and to the name Bernardo Jacinto. But the lead looked like a dead end – there was no proof that Jacinto and Ferreira were the same person; and, even if they were, it didn't make it any easier to trace Ferreira.

'And there's another thing,' Bergerac went on. 'Barney Crozier's breathing down my neck. He thinks we're wasting police resources, quote unquote. What he means is that finding Ferreira won't help the arrests quota.'

'And what do you think, Jim?' Susan asked.

He shrugged. 'The same as I always thought. The odds are that Ferreira's had a drop too much. He'll be back – with his tail between his legs.' He turned to Lil. 'I'm sorry, but there's a limit to what we can do in a case like this. It's not as if Ferreira's under age or mixed up in a crime.'

Lil sipped her white wine. 'I was talking to Jean-Luc this afternoon. You know Alvaro fainted? It was just after he'd served someone.'

'So?'

'Jean-Luc wondered if there was a connection.'

'Did the man show signs of recognizing Ferreira?'

'Not that I know of. Alvaro shouldn't have been serving him, in fact. Jean-Luc took the order and passed it on to young Jamie – it was one of his tables. But Jamie was under pressure, so Alvaro took the drink over.'

Bergerac sighed. Their glasses were empty: he signalled to the barman. At that moment a phone rang somewhere behind the long, marble-topped counter.

Well-meaning members of the public were a mixed blessing for a policeman. Especially when they buttonholed you when you were meant to be off duty. He caught Susan's eye and realized that she would be hurt on Lil's behalf if he didn't go through the motions of being interested.

'Did Jean-Luc recognize the bloke?'

'Didn't know him from Adam.' Lil smiled apologetically. 'Look. I know this is a bore for you, Jim. I'm sorry. The man was middle-aged. Thickset. Wanted a large Bell's. Looked like a small-time businessman.'

The barman coughed loudly. 'Would you be Detective Sergeant Bergerac, by any chance?'

Bergerac agreed that he would.

'Someone wants you on the phone.' He indicated the empty glasses. 'Same again?'

It was a short phone call. Bergerac's face was grim as he returned to the table.

'I won't have another drink,' he told the barman. 'Just the wine for the ladies, OK?'

Susan looked up at him. 'Trouble?'

'I'm afraid so. I've got to go. That was Barry Goddard. I told him I'd be here.' He glanced at Lil. 'I had him and Peggy run a check on your friend Alvaro.'

'He's got a record?' Lil said.

'Alvaro Ferreira hasn't,' Bergerac said. 'But Bernardo Jacinto has done time for petty theft. He's a Portuguese waiter whose last known address is in Catford. But he isn't there now. At present he's wanted for the murder of his wife.'

Alice Crozier answered the door. 'Oh, it's you,' she said, without enthusiasm. 'Can't it wait? We're in the middle of dinner.'

'I'm sorry, Alice,' Bergerac said, untruthfully. 'It's urgent. I need a word with Barney now.'

'I suppose you'd better come in.'

She showed him into the sitting room. The curtains concealed the big picture window which overlooked the sea. In one corner the video was purring away beneath the blank screen of the television. Bergerac glanced at his watch and then at the channel the video was recording. He made the interesting discovery that someone in the Crozier household was a fan of *EastEnders*. It was interesting because both Barney and Alice made no secret of their intellectual pretensions. Maybe they watched *EastEnders* for sociological reasons.

Crozier appeared in the doorway; he was in his shirt-sleeves and had a napkin in his hands.

'I hope you've got a good reason for this,' he said.

'I want authorization to go to London first thing tomorrow,' Bergerac said.

'You'll need a bloody good reason for that, too.'

'It's Ferreira. We – '

'Ferreira? I thought I told you – '

'Hang on, Barney.' Bergerac sat down. 'Ferreira is either connected with or identical to a bloke called Bernardo Jacinto. Jacinto's another Portuguese waiter. The Met have been looking for him since 13 October.'

Crozier frowned. 'Why?'

'That's when they found the body of his wife. Someone had cut her up with a carving knife. And they rather think it was him.'

'I see.' Crozier perched on the arm of a chair. 'And if Jacinto's really Ferreira . . .?'

Bergerac nodded. 'It's more than likely he's still on the island.'

Crozier's stern face dissolved into a smile. 'So he'd be our pigeon. A major arrest for the Bureau. I like it, Jim. That'd keep Hungerford quiet for a bit.'

'For about five minutes, I should think,' Bergerac said. 'But we're jumping the gun. Lil's going to get me a photo of Alvaro from her personal records. Before we do anything else we need a positive ID.'

'We could wire a print to London.' Crozier hesitated. 'But on the other hand, I see your point. A personal visit might achieve more.'

Bergerac smothered a smile. If they wired the photo, the Met would do the ID and the Met would take a little more of the credit.

'Who's in charge at that end?' Crozier asked.

'Nominally, it's Detective Superintendent Overstone. But I gather that the man to see is an old DS called Tuffnell. He's done most of the donkey-work.'

'Tuffnell?' Crozier said. 'Hasn't he made inspector yet? I met him on a course at Hendon once. Bit of a weirdo.' Crozier stopped. Suddenly he slapped his thigh. 'Got it!'

'Eh?'

'It's nothing, really.' He grinned unexpectedly, reminding Bergerac of the much younger Barney Crozier he had once known. 'Even so, it's been bugging me for hours. I saw a bloke whose face I knew in St Aubin this afternoon. But I just couldn't place him. Now I've remembered: Hendon.'

'So he's a copper?'

'He was on the same course as me and Tuffnell. Must be ten years ago. Now what was his name? Ronny something. Pine? No – it was Quine. I'm sure of it.'

Bergerac could not resist the temptation. 'Do you think he's poaching?'

Crozier was perpetually on guard against unauthorized police operations on his patch. Even when they were authorized he found them hard to accept. Anything which threatened his autonomy was anathema to him.

'Good God, you might be right.'

'Or perhaps he was on holiday,' Bergerac suggested.

'At this time of year?' Crozier rubbed his chin. 'But maybe you've got a point – he might be with a woman.'

'A dirty weekend?' Bergerac said with a straight face.

Crozier looked disapprovingly at him.

'Of course,' Bergerac went on, 'ten years is a long time. He might have left the force by now.'

'See if you can find out tomorrow,' Crozier said. 'Discreetly – don't make a big deal out of it. I know: give Tuffnell my regards and ask him if he sees anything of Ronny Quine these days.'

A few hours later Ronny Quine was crouching beside a dustbin and trying to imagine he was warm.

It was a filthy night – not quite as cold as it had been; but the rain and the wind made up for that. The leather jacket protected his body but his head and legs were soaked.

Physical discomfort was only one of his worries. He wasn't on home ground: he didn't know how the police patrols operated in St Helier; and this island was too damn small for anyone who wanted to evade them in a hurry.

The geography was another problem. A really thorough recce had been out of the question because one of the waiters might recall his face. True, he remembered a certain amount from the other night. Norma had been inside for a drink earlier this evening, and she'd managed to learn a little more about the layout upstairs on the excuse that she was trying to find the ladies' loo.

At least he knew the outside. There were three entrances, two of them here at the back. He had seen the last of the patrons leave half an hour ago at the front. The head-waiter had locked and bolted the doors, which meant that the staff would probably come out of the ground-floor door at the back.

The third entrance was the fire-escape door at first-floor level. The fire escape itself was dimly illuminated by an outside light. Down here in the yard half a dozen cars were parked. The row of dustbins was fortunately in shadow.

It was too damn risky. It was all very well for Norma Jean to say that the rewards were worth the risks – she was probably asleep by now; and she was certainly warm and dry wherever she was.

Wherever she was – for all he knew, she was keeping warm and dry with Oliver. Quine had noticed the way that Oliver looked at her. He had no illusions about Norma's definition of fidelity. It was difficult to imagine her in bed with the fat boy. But who needed sex appeal when you were rich?

The screech of an unoiled hinge jerked Quine out of his self-pity. A slab of light shot out from the ground-floor doorway. One by one, the staff emerged. The cars nosed out of the yard.

Two cars were left. A well-preserved middle-aged woman climbed into one of them. She rolled down the window.

'Hop in, Jamie,' she said. 'I'll give you a lift.'

A youth ran round to the passenger side of the car.

'Jean-Luc?' she called across the yard to an older man who was locking the door. 'Are the lights off in the cellar?'

'Yes, madame. I checked.'

The woman drove away. Jean-Luc turned off the outside light. As he climbed into his car, he was whistling tunelessly through his teeth. Quine had a bad moment when the engine failed to fire. The starter motor whirred again, and the engine gave a reassuring roar. Jean-Luc revved it for a few seconds, filling the yard with exhaust fumes. At last he drove away.

It looked hopeful, Quine thought. That snatch of conversation suggested that no one else was inside. In the unlikely event that a place as small as this had a night watchman, it would be his job to take care of the lights and the locking-up.

Quine forced himself to wait. He pulled the stocking over his head, reducing his features to a blur. He decided to count slowly to five hundred. The yard was completely dark. All he could hear were the muted sounds of a few cars on the main road.

Fifty-eight, fifty-nine, sixty . . .

It all depended on the burglar alarm – or alarms. The odds were that the alarm wouldn't be too sophisticated somewhere like this – in which case he could cope with it himself; it was just a matter of identifying the pressure pads and avoiding – or, if necessary, disconnecting – them.

Eighty-nine, ninety, ninety-one . . .

But once inside he couldn't afford to waste time. There might be a less obvious secondary system. If there were, it all came down to the speed of the police response. This wasn't London: the distances were smaller and the police force less tightly stretched. Once inside, he decided, he would allow himself five minutes and no more. If Norma was right, the files had to be in one of two offices. And they should be obvious, too – there was no reason to lock them in the safe or conceal them.

Hundred and twelve, hundred and thirteen . . .

'Is there any news of Alvaro?' Jamie asked.

Lil changed down for a corner. 'Nothing certain,' she said noncommittally. Bergerac had asked her to keep quiet about the possible link between Alvaro Ferreira and Bernardo Jacinto. 'But the police are looking into it. I expect he'll turn up soon.' Suddenly her hands tightened on the steering wheel. 'Oh *damn*!'

'What's up?' Jamie said.

'It's Alvaro. I've just remembered something I left in the office. I'll have to go back.'

Lil braked and drew up outside the small terraced house where Jamie still lived with his parents.

'I'm sorry,' he said shyly, as he fumbled for the door handle.

'No, I'm glad I remembered.' Lil grinned at him in the darkness, realizing his shyness had as much to do with her sex as with the fact that she was his employer. At her age it was a compliment. 'Thanks for reminding me.'

Four hundred and thirty-six, four hundred and thirty-seven –

On the main road, a car slowed. Its engine grew louder. Quine stopped counting. He stiffened and cocked his head to listen. A trickle of rain-water ran down his neck.

The water was the least of his worries. The car drew nearer. He felt in his pocket for the thick, rubber truncheon Norma had given him. Headlights surged into the yard, briefly touching the line of dustbins and picking out the glistening black zigzag of the fire escape.

The police? Maybe one of the staff had noticed him? Quine got ready to run. He measured with his eyes the best escape route. He could dodge behind the incoming car and reach the lane in a few seconds. They'd expect him to make for the main road; instead he'd use the footpath. His chance of getting away was perhaps fifty-fifty. There were too many ifs and buts to consider. He swore soundlessly at Norma for getting him into this.

The car pulled into the yard, splashing through the puddles on the rutted surface, and stopped with a jerk. The engine died but the headlights stayed on; the rain fell like silver needles through their beams.

The driver's door opened. The courtesy light came on automatically. Quine grunted with surprise. It was only the woman. And she was alone.

The woman ran through the rain to the ground-floor door. She unlocked it and slipped inside.

Quine was moving almost before he realized what a gift the gods had given him. He slipped across the yard. The drumming of the rain masked his footsteps.

The stupid cow had left the door ajar. Inside, the light was on. The woman was standing on tiptoe, trying to insert a key in a red box mounted high on the wall.

'Oh, come on!' she said to herself. 'Damn it, I haven't got all night!'

Quine hung back. The alarm system probably operated with a thirty-second time-lag, to give legitimate users of the building an opportunity to switch it off once they were inside.

The truncheon was heavy in the palm of his gloved hand. He edged towards the door.

There was a click and a sigh of relief: the alarm must now be out of action. A second later, he heard the clack of high heels on an uncarpeted surface.

Quine darted inside. A long corridor lay ahead. The woman was maybe ten yards away, walking briskly. Abandoning subtlety, he charged after her. His shoes squelched and slapped as he ran.

The woman turned. Her face was blank with shock. No hat to worry about. That amount of hair wouldn't cushion the blow. Quine raised the truncheon. *It's easy!* he thought joyfully. *As easy as falling off a log.*

But the thought was premature. The woman suddenly sidestepped. The truncheon missed her by inches. Quine, braced for the impact, was thrown briefly off-balance.

The woman swung her handbag round in a wide arc. It caught him full on the cheekbone. The edge of the buckle cut through the nylon and dug into his skin. Quine grunted with pain.

But the buckle snagged on the stocking mask. The woman held on to the handbag for a second too long. Quine clouted her with his left hand. She reeled away and slumped against the wall.

Everything was easy again. Quine laughed as he moved cautiously towards her.

He raised the truncheon.

'No,' the woman said. 'Look, there's no need –'

Then at last she was silent and still.

CHAPTER

11

The beard was growing again.

As he walked through the rain and the darkness, down from St Saviour to St Helier, he was bitterly conscious of the impression he must make if anyone chanced to see him. Crossing a field, he had slipped; the whole of his left side was a smear of mud. Bits of straw from the barn still stuck to his clothes. So did the farmyard smell – though that, thank God, was less noticeable in the open air.

The bristle irritated his chin. Usually he had to shave twice a day. Customers and employers did not like to see stubble on your face. In his other life, that was the reason he had originally had a beard. It saved so much time and effort.

He tried not to think about the reason for removing the beard – such a smart little imperial; distinguished and charmingly old-fashioned, it was always earning him compliments from the ladies; and Caterina had liked it too.

Caterina. The memory hurt. It always would. And now, since the man he knew as Ronny had arrived, fear was mixed with the pain. If Ronny was here, the woman must be with him. She was even worse. It was she who had held the knife. During the last twenty-four hours, he had been so afraid that he had seriously considered throwing himself on the mercy of the police.

The country lane changed imperceptibly into a suburban highway. A dog barked as he passed a large house, set back from the road. He had never been here before, but he knew roughly where he was. In the last few weeks he had spent most of his leisure time walking in and around St Helier. Walking helped to dull the pain.

What mercy could the police show him in this cold, indifferent land? They didn't hang you here: they locked you up and threw away the key. He knew what went on in prison; he knew what the other inmates did to little men who had been convicted of savagely murdering their wives. Capital punishment was more merciful than that.

Fear and pain changed you in so many ways; you could not predict the effects they would have. He had thought himself a civilized man – a citizen of the modern world, who had outgrown the barbarism of his ancestors along with their superstitions.

But now he knew that Jorge had been right. Jorge was a good boy: his cousin had believed him; he had sheltered him; he had found him another identity; and he had even come down to Portsmouth to see him off to Jersey on the ferry.

It was then, at the docks, that Jorge had said it: *There is only one way to be free again. Free in your heart, Bernardo. The old way. Like our grandfather did to the man who lay with his sister.*

Eusebio Ferreira had left the women of the village to deal with his sister; naturally she was forever defiled. He reserved the man for himself. He took the ancient muzzle-loading gun he used for shooting duck. First he mutilated the adulterer; then, a little later, he shot him in the head. The village produced half a dozen willing witnesses to swear that the adulterer had killed himself accidentally while cleaning his double-barrelled shotgun.

By now Bernardo had reached the bottom of St Saviour's Hill. A police car came towards him, its light flashing. He slipped into the shelter of the driveway which led up to the Hotel de France. His heart seemed to hammer in his chest.

This was a rich man's island, he thought: the poor and the derelict were automatically suspect.

The car passed him. He resumed his journey. It must be after four o'clock. He crossed the road and turned into a side street. Ahead, to his left, he could see the great towers of the gas-works. Soon he turned again, just before the pagan majesty of the Masonic Temple. He was back in Oxford Road.

The old way. There was only one anaesthetic for fear and pain: revenge. Old Eusebio had known: when there was nothing else to live for, you had to travel by the old way or go down into the darkness for ever.

Carlton House loomed up ahead. He glanced up at the uncurtained window of his old room. At least he would never sleep there again. He was free of the smells and the dirt and the ceaseless clack of Mrs Le Davre's tongue.

His destination was on the other side of the road. He scarcely knew why he had investigated the house opposite. Mrs Le Davre had mentioned in one of her vitriolic monologues that it was empty; the owners lived there only in the summer; in the winter they went to Majorca. They were so rich, Mrs Le Davre complained, they didn't even bother to let the house. But they paid her an absurdly small sum to keep an eye on their summer home and to keep it clean and aired; the wealthy, she said, were always mean.

In his old life, Bernardo would not have hesitated. He had jettisoned the old superstitious prohibition against stealing; it was not appropriate for a modern man. If life gave you an opportunity, it was foolish not to take it. Nothing big – for that increased the risks to an unacceptable level. But trifles were another matter: a little here, a little there – it all added up to a useful supplement to a married man's income.

But his old life had ended when a miscalculation landed him in prison with a six-month sentence, reduced by a third for good behaviour. Those four months had destroyed his confidence in the virtues of modern man. And, indirectly, they had led to Caterina's death.

Still, almost without thinking, he had absorbed the details which Mrs Le Davre had so prodigally given him: the location of Mrs Le Davre's key to the back door of the empty house; the routine which turned off the burglar alarm; and the big freezer in the cellar which the owners kept well-stocked for their return in the spring.

Bernardo had made a copy of the key. One night, after work, he had slipped inside the house. He had taken nothing – in fact there was little to steal that he could sell or use.

Oxford Road was empty. Bernardo leant against the wall for a moment. There was no sign of life.

A gate blocked the covered alley which led to the back door. It seemed locked – but all you needed was a pencil or a twig to lift the latch on the inside. It was child's play.

He crept along the passage and let himself into the house. Perhaps he should have come here last night; but at the time the shock of seeing Ronny had stopped him thinking properly – he had been conscious of nothing except the desperate need to escape. Now his mind was clearer and he knew what he had to do. No one would search for him in this place: it was too close to Carlton House. Here he could have food and warmth – and even alcohol.

Here he could wait as the hunter waits in his hide for the tiger.

And when the tiger comes?

Bernardo climbed the stairs. His night vision was good. On the landing he went through the first doorway on the left. It gave on to a small room, furnished like a man's study, with bookshelves and hunting prints arrayed on the walls and heavy armchairs drawn up around the empty fireplace.

Beneath the window was a desk. Bernardo opened the shallow central drawer over the well. His fingers touched an envelope, which chinked as he moved it aside; it contained the old man's campaign medals, his cap badge and his insignia of rank. Once Bernardo would have laughed at such evidence of sentimentality. At the back of the drawer was a bundle wrapped in a threadbare towel.

It was still here, thank God. Bernardo laid the bundle on the blotter and gently unwrapped it. He smelled the oil and felt it on his hands. The old man looked after his possessions.

Six cartridges rolled on to the blotter. Then he touched the Webley itself – the standard-issue revolver of a British officer in World War II. The butt fitted snugly into his hand. The weight surprised him. He ran his finger along the barrel. Times had changed: this was better than a muzzle-loading duck gun; old Eusebio would have approved.

When the tiger comes, the hunter shoots him.

Sergeant Corrance took the call.

'All right,' he said with a yawn. 'I'll send a car down.' He scribbled down the details and glanced at his watch: half an hour to go before the end of the nightshift. 'Eh? You want an ambulance as well?'

A woman's voice crackled angrily at the other end of the phone.

Corrance sighed. 'I heard you.'

This time the voice was quieter. Corrance rubbed his fat, white face and thought longingly of breakfast and bed.

'Bergerac?' he said when she had finished. 'You mean Jim Bergerac, at the Bureau des Etrangers? Why does she want him told? I mean, I presume this woman's a resident . . . Oh, I get it. Personal friend, eh? . . . All right, I didn't mean to imply . . . Goodbye.'

Corrance lit a cigarette. Still smarting from the lash of his caller's eloquence, he arranged for the dispatch of a car and an ambulance. The woman had identified herself as a cleaner. All he could say was that she could clean up her manners, and no mistake.

Finally he dialled Bergerac's home number. Corrance hoped that the call would wake him up – he had better things to do than personal favours for the Bureau's girl-friends. To his disappointment, the phone was answered on the second ring.

'Bergerac.'

'Morning, Jim. Tom Corrance here. Not got you up, I hope? We've just had a call from a cleaner at one of the nightclubs. What's its name? Ah yes – Lil's Place.'

'They've had a break-in?'

'So it seems. The owner got knocked on the head and stuffed in a broom cupboard. Seems she's been asking for you. Personal, like.'

'Is she in hospital yet?'

'No,' Corrance said. He added smugly: 'But I've sent an ambulance over.'

The line went dead.

Corrance blew a raspberry at the handset. Bergerac might have troubled to thank him. Those swollen-headed Bureau boys were all the same: thought they were God's gift to the Jersey States Police.

He looked at his watch once more: twenty-five minutes until the end of his shift.

There is a 20 m.p.h. speed limit in St Helier but Bergerac temporarily suspended it.

At this time of morning there was hardly any traffic. The Triumph Roadster responded happily to the challenge. A few minutes later Bergerac drove into the yard behind the nightclub. A squad car was already there, its radio chattering away to itself. Lil's car was parked beyond it. The ambulance had not arrived.

PC Yardley was waiting for him. 'Hello, Sarge. Corrance said you were on your way.'

The red-haired constable was clearly relieved to see him. He led Bergerac along the corridor and up the stairs.

'She's upstairs in her office,' Yardley said. 'Lying on a sofa there.'

'You moved her?' Bergerac said with a frown.

'She moved herself, Sarge. She was conscious when the cleaners found her.' He indicated a door. 'In there.'

Bergerac poked his head inside the tiny, windowless room. An unshaded bulb dangled from the ceiling. It was here that the cleaners kept the tools of their trade. The floor was concrete. The temperature was noticeably lower than in the corridor.

He glanced quickly at the door. There was no lock: it was held in place by two heavy bolts on the outside.

'Chummy had it easy,' Yardley said. 'As far as we can see, he was waiting at the back, ready to break in when the place was empty. The owner came back unexpectedly for something. She turned off the burglar alarm. He sneaked in behind her and knocked her out.'

'Did she get a look at him?' Bergerac asked as they climbed the stairs.

'Heavy bloke in a black leather jacket. Wore a stocking over his head.'

Bergerac paused at the top of the stairs. 'It was raining. Did he leave any footprints?'

Yardley shook his head. 'He cleaned up after him. When he put her in that room he picked up a bucket and mop. A cool customer, whoever he is.'

'What did he take?'

'We're not sure yet. One of the cleaners thinks some Scotch has gone from the bar, plus a couple of cartons of cigarettes. There was no money lying around. The safe hasn't been touched.'

The door to Lil's office was open. An electric fan-heater was on at full blast. Lil had her feet up on the sofa and a mug of tea in her hand. She was alarmingly pale, though there was no obvious sign of a wound on her head. The elderly cleaners were fussing over her like two hens with one chick. A young constable stood by the door, staring at his boots. The cleaners had given him a mug of tea as well.

Bergerac smiled at Lil. 'You been in the wars again?'

'I gave as good as I got,' she said. 'Well, nearly. I swiped him with my handbag. He might have a bruise on his face.' She looked sternly at him. 'You should have had a shave before you came to visit a lady.'

Her voice was strong and her sense of humour was undamaged; but Bergerac sensed that she was still in a state of shock. He took her gently through what had happened.

'It's all your fault,' she said afterwards. 'I only came back for that photo.'

'Ferreira's?'

She nodded. 'I was going to drop it off at the Bureau on my way home. You'd better get it now. It's over there. The top drawer.'

She pointed to one of the filing cabinets behind her desk. Simultaneously Bergerac heard the siren of an ambulance.

'There's your taxi, Lil.'

'I don't need an ambulance,' she said. 'I'm fine. Really, there's no point in me going to hospital.'

'You don't have any choice,' Bergerac said. He nodded at the younger constable. 'Go and let them in. They'll need a stretcher.'

'That's right,' one of the cleaners agreed. 'You do as the sergeant says, dear, and no argy-bargy.'

'Delayed reaction,' her colleague added darkly. 'I've seen it all before. The sooner you're in hospital, the better.'

'But I must phone Jean-Luc,' Lil said in dismay. 'I need to sort out – '

'I'll phone him,' Bergerac told her. 'You don't need to do anything, OK?'

The drawer was unlocked. It contained A to M of the personnel records, arranged in hanging files. Bergerac lifted out the folder labelled F and leafed through it.

'It's not here,' he said.

Lil frowned. 'It must be. I had it only the other day. And I doubt if it's misfiled – my secretary's manic about putting things in their proper places.'

The heavy tread of the ambulance men was on the stairs.

Bergerac flicked through the Gs without success. But at last he found Ferreira's folder at the back of the Es. It included a passport-sized photograph of the little waiter, stapled to his letter of application.

'Do you mind if I take the whole thing?'

'You can take the kitchen sink for all I care.' Lil rubbed her forehead. 'Maybe you're right about going into hospital.'

The ambulance men came into the room.

Bergerac bent and kissed her cheek. 'I have to go. I'll call Jean-Luc from the Bureau. And I'll tell Susan, too. If I can, I'll look in this evening.'

Lil caught his hand. 'Jim – I've got a feeling about all this. That man who attacked me – he's dangerous. *Really* dangerous.'

He tried to keep his voice light: 'The famous womanly intuition?'

'You can call it what you want.' Her face was haggard under the remains of yesterday's make-up. 'But you'll promise me one thing? Please? You'll take care?'

*

'I don't care what Crozier said.' Bergerac tapped the file on the desk. 'This changes everything, Barry.'

Goddard took a sip of coffee. 'It's your decision. But the Chief Inspector wanted me to get that report on his desk by lunchtime.'

'It'll have to wait. I'll leave a message for him with Peggy. He'll understand. Anything'll get his blessing if it might lead to an arrest.'

'It's a bit of a long shot, isn't it?'

Bergerac sighed. 'Got any other explanation? It's obviously a professional job – rubber cosh, stocking mask; he cleaned up after him; he was patient enough to wait for the right time – even turned on the burglar alarm when he left. So why does he just take a bottle of Glenlivet and a few hundred cigarettes?'

'Maybe he tried the safe but – '

'If that bloke had tried the safe, he'd've cracked it. Or at least left his calling card on it. No, he wanted to make it look like an amateur break-in.'

'But you can't prove he was after Ferreira's file, can you?'

'Got a better idea? If Lil's right about her secretary, it shouldn't have been misfiled. But the attacker might easily have slipped it in the wrong place. He was in a hurry, remember. He wouldn't have had the light on, either. Probably just a torch. The office window overlooks the road.'

'All right, Jim. Say he was after Ferreira's file, for the sake of argument. I still don't see why – '

'Barry – just listen, will you? Jean-Luc thinks Ferreira fainted after seeing a mystery man at the nightclub. A mystery man tries to get Ferreira's file. He doesn't steal it: he just looks at it. It seems that someone else is after Ferreira besides the police. If Ferreira's Jacinto, then his

CV is probably a pack of lies. But one bit of information's accurate: his present address.'

'So you want me to sit outside Carlton House in an unmarked car until further notice? Great. And what happens if I see a middle-aged, broad-shouldered mystery man, maybe with a bruise on his face?'

'You tail him,' Bergerac said. 'If he breaks the law, you nick him. And maybe – just maybe – he'll lead us to Ferreira.'

CHAPTER
12

Detective Superintendent Overstone looked younger than Bergerac but he acted as if he were twenty years older.

'Well, Sergeant,' he said slowly. 'What it boils down to is this. You think this chap' – he held up the enlarged photograph of Alvaro Ferreira – 'might be Jacinto. Unfortunately' – he sniffed – 'you've mislaid Ferreira, so you can't haul him in and find out for certain.'

Overstone was standing by the window, looking down at the traffic which rumbled along Victoria Street, between the railway terminus and Westminster. So far he had avoided making eye-contact with his visitor. His room was large, airy and anonymous. Its only distinguishing feature was the pervasive smell of Chanel Pour Monsieur.

'Yes, sir,' Bergerac murmured as respectfully as he could; Overstone was merely repeating what Bergerac had just told him, albeit in slightly different words. 'But, as I said, it's probable he's still on Jersey.'

'But you don't *know* that, do you?' Overstone said with the air of a man who has made an unanswerable point. 'It's all a bit too hypothetical for my liking.'

'It's a fair assumption, sir. We keep a pretty close eye on who comes in and who goes out. It's not as if Ferreira – or Jacinto – had any known contacts on the island.'

'Then why haven't you traced him already?'

'Because it was only yesterday that we found out about the Jacinto connection. Until then Ferreira was just another missing person.'

Overstone fingered the trouser crease of his pinstriped suit. Together with the cream silk shirt, the fashionable tie and the slim gold wristwatch, the suit made him look like a rising young commodities broker – the sort of man who would be more at home in a Porsche than a police car.

'Ferreira,' he said almost to himself. 'Now why does that name sound familiar?' He shrugged the question away and raised his voice: 'So what exactly do you want to do, Sergeant?'

'Try to establish if Ferreira is Jacinto. Then, if he is, we'd be very grateful if we could see the file on him.'

The servility did not come easily to Bergerac, but he knew he could not afford to antagonize Overstone. A Detective Superintendent in the Met was a powerful man, especially where one of his own cases was concerned.

Overstone sat down behind the desk. He opened his Filofax and consulted the diary section. There was a silence during which he pursed his lips as if he were in the throes of a difficult mental calculation. Bergerac knew better than to interrupt the Superintendent's train of thought. Senior officers' silences were inviolable.

'I've a meeting with the AC in twenty minutes,' Overstone said at last.

Bergerac tried to look suitably impressed.

'I suppose you could have a word with my DS – if he's in the building. He can brief you. After all, it's nothing very complicated. A simple case of matrimonial homicide.'

Bergerac cleared his throat. 'That would be very kind, sir.'

'I hope your superiors in the States Police are equally grateful.' Overstone inspected his manicured fingernails. 'I have sometimes found them – how can I put it? – a little less than eager to cooperate with us.'

For the first time, the Superintendent's hard blue eyes stared unblinkingly across the desk at his visitor. It was quite simple, Bergerac thought with a spurt of distaste: he'll scratch our back if we'll scratch his. It was easy to guess what Overstone wanted: a lot of money circulated through the financial mazes of Jersey and a percentage of it came from criminal sources on the mainland; the Bureau des Etrangers had rather more leverage than the Met over Jersey's financial institutions. From his point of view, such assistance was considerably more valuable than the arrest of a petty thief turned wife-killer. Not that Overstone would forgo the lion's share of the credit: he was too shrewd for that.

Overstone picked up one of his telephones and punched an internal number.

'Tuffnell? A Detective Sergeant Bergerac of the Jersey States Police is on his way down to you.'

'It'll be my pleasure, sir.' The sarcasm in the tinny voice on the other end of the line was perfectly audible on Bergerac's side of the desk.

Overstone frowned. 'They may have a lead on the Jacinto case. See if there's anything in it, will you?' He replaced the handset. 'Sordid business, Sergeant. Makes one wish we still had capital punishment, eh?'

'He has to be at home,' Norma Jean said impatiently. 'He's got nowhere else to go.'

Quine nodded. 'Too scared to go to work. I'd've seen him last night if he'd been there. He's keeping his head down and hoping for the best.'

'We'd better wait till this evening. Until we've put the babies to bed.'

Norma Jean Veldman poured herself another cup of coffee and lit her first cigarette of the day. Usually they breakfasted earlier, but both of them needed to sleep late after the excitements of last night. It meant that the babies hadn't had their breakfast yet, but that didn't matter: they'd survive.

She had a feeling about this business: the pieces were beginning to fall into place. Her increasing optimism even went some way to reconciling her with their surroundings.

They were sitting in the saloon of the big cabin-cruiser which was moored in the inlet. Inside it was as comfortable as most hotel suites and at least the drinks were free; the old man was evidently fond of his luxuries. She disliked intensely the fact that they were floating on the water, but she knew it could have been much worse. The inlet was so sheltered that it translated the roughest weather from the Channel into a gentle swell. Nevertheless, she was practically living on tablets designed to stave off seasickness. Better safe than sorry.

Quine leant back and picked his teeth. 'Shame about the woman. I might have been able to get in and out without anyone knowing.'

Norma Jean shrugged. 'Yes and no. You might have run into problems with the alarm. It's not as if they can know what we wanted. On balance I think we were lucky.'

There were footsteps on deck and they fell silent. Oliver burst into the cabin. He wore a dripping oilskin. His face was pink with exertion.

'Haven't they had their breakfast yet?' he demanded.

Norma poured him a cup of coffee. 'There's no hurry, Oliver dear.' She glanced at Quine and was pleased to note that he found the endearment distasteful. 'We had a late night.'

She batted her eyelashes at Quine; he grinned at her with obvious relief. Men were such children, she thought; you could send their emotional barometers up and down like yo-yos. Oliver was in many ways the better long-term prospect; but at present she couldn't do without Ronny. She would have to put Oliver on hold.

Oliver stripped off his oilskin and sat down. Norma passed him his coffee, leaning forward considerately so he could catch a glimpse of her cleavage; that would give him something to be going on with.

'When will you call today?' he asked.

'Sometime this morning,' Norma said. 'It's my turn, I think. Oh, by the way, we'll need a car again this evening. That's OK, isn't it?'

Oliver licked his lips. 'I was going out myself, actually. Someone should stay here to keep an eye on the babies.'

'We need a break,' Quine growled. 'I'll go round the twist if I stay here much longer. I'm not a bloody seagull.'

'The babies'll be quite safe,' Norma said. 'I mean, it's not as if they can go anywhere.'

Oliver glanced at her and then at Quine. 'All right,' he said. He knew as well as they did that he wasn't in a position to insist. 'I'll stay here tonight.'

Generous in victory, Norma smiled at him and allowed her leg to touch his beneath the table.

'We'll make it up to you,' she said huskily. 'I promise.'

'It's like a dream,' John Danston said. 'It's all a bad dream. So it doesn't matter.'

'That's my boy.' The woman chuckled. It was a sensuous sound, which made Danston feel faintly uncomfortable. 'And in the dream, the Pilsen's tender looks pretty damn fine, doesn't it?'

'No,' Danston said. 'I mean yes.'

'Think positive, darling. Like your Emma does.'

'I *need* Emma.'

'I know you do. And she'll be back – after the meeting. I promise.'

'Can you give her a message? Say that I love her and – '

There was a click and the line went dead.

The tears rolled slowly down John Danston's cheeks.

*

Detective Sergeant Gordon Tuffnell put down the phone.

'I owe you a drink,' he said. 'The lads downstairs confirmed it. Come on.'

Bergerac didn't move from his chair. He had spent the last hour kicking his heels in a waiting room. Tuffnell had only just condescended to see him. So far the only thing he'd said was that he'd buy Bergerac a drink if there was anything in his story; the tone of his voice had suggested he didn't think it likely.

'The prints on the frame match?'

Tuffnell nodded. 'And Forensic made a positive ID from the photo, too. So we can rule out the idea that Jacinto just happened to handle the frame you found in Ferreira's room: they're the same person, and that's official. Let's go and find that pint.'

'It'll be a pint of orange squash in my case,' Bergerac said. He stood up and pulled on his leather jacket.

Tuffnell raised his eyebrows. 'You don't approve of drinking on duty?'

'It's not that. I'm an alcoholic.'

'Ah, well.' Tuffnell grinned. 'That explains it. A pint of orange squash it is.'

It was then that Bergerac decided he liked Gordie Tuffnell. It was always instructive to see how people reacted when you said you were an alcoholic. Some were embarrassed, as if you'd sworn in church; some pretended not to have heard you; some fell over themselves not to lead you into temptation. Best of all, in Bergerac's opinion, were the minority who accepted what you said and carried on as normal.

It was a little after 11.30. The pub was one of those seedy back-street establishments that exist even in the smartest areas of London. Half a dozen drinkers were already there. They took one look at Tuffnell and thereafter gave him and Bergerac a wide berth.

'They know me here,' Tuffnell said comfortably as they stood at the bar. The barmaid gave them precedence over the other people waiting to be served. 'God knows, it's one of the few perks we've got.'

He ordered their drinks and a couple of rounds of sandwiches. They sat down at a table near the fire. An elderly man was already at the table. He smiled ingratiatingly at Tuffnell and scuttled away to the other end of the room.

Tuffnell took a long pull of his drink and wiped his mouth with the back of his hand. 'What did His Nibs tell you?'

'Overstone? Not much. I gathered he thought the case was just a minor domestic squabble.'

'The man's a fool,' Tuffnell said dispassionately. 'Which means he'll probably end up Assistant Commissioner. Can't see further than his career.' Without warning he switched tack: 'What I'd like to know is why Jacinto's gone missing again.'

Bergerac shrugged. 'I don't know for certain but I think he saw a man he knew.'

'Where?'

'At the nightclub where he worked.' Bergerac hesitated. 'The club was burgled last night. The owner got in the way and was coshed.'

Tuffnell stared into his drink. 'Much taken?'

'No. They tried to make it look an amateur break-in, but I don't think it was. My guess is that they wanted a look at Jacinto's file.'

The old man was quick to see the point: 'His address?'

'That was my guess too.'

'So someone else is after Bernardo. It makes sense.'

'Are you going to tell me?' Bergerac asked.

'I suppose I might as well. It's one in the eye for

Overstone, if nothing else. I never liked the matrimonial-dispute theory.'

'Why not?'

Tuffnell stared into the fire. 'Jacinto's a petty thief, that's all. He was a waiter in a hotel restaurant, you know. Pinched a bit of cash from a few bedrooms – that sort of thing. I had a word with the bloke who nicked him. He said Jacinto wouldn't say boo to a goose. A mild little man.'

'So was Crippen,' Bergerac said, determined to play devil's advocate.

'Yes, I know.' Tuffnell frowned. 'And then there's the painting of his missis. He ordered it before the murder, right? But he picked it up afterwards. Why? It doesn't make sense. You don't want a picture to remind you of someone you just sliced to death. The neighbours, incidentally, say that the Jacintos were devoted to one another.'

'Neighbours can be wrong.'

Tuffnell gave no sign of having heard him. 'And then there's the Ferreira business. The real Ferreira.'

'Who's he when he's at home?'

'Jorge Ferreira. Another immigrant waiter here in London. I ran a check on him and his family, with a little help from Interpol. Turns out that Jorge's Jacinto's cousin. More than that, his elder brother's name is Alvaro. And guess where Alvaro is. Six feet down in a Lisbon cemetery. He and his moped got into an argument with an articulated lorry.'

'I get it,' Bergerac said slowly. 'After Caterina's murder, Bernardo runs to Jorge. Jorge lets him use Alvaro's identity. I need to see Jorge.'

'Any time you like.' Tuffnell emptied his glass. 'But I doubt if you'll get much out of him. He's in the mortuary. Your round, I think.'

Bergerac looked up sharply. 'What happened?'

'They found him last night,' Tuffnell said. 'In the boot of

a stolen car in the long-stay car park at Heathrow. He'd been strangled. But before that, someone had been redesigning his hands. With an electric drill.'

The barmaid arrived with their sandwiches just as Bergerac lost his appetite. He fetched Tuffnell another drink. By the time he returned to their table, Tuffnell had gobbled his own round and was eyeing Bergerac's. Bergerac pushed the plate towards him.

'Like the break-in last night,' he said. 'A professional job.'

Tuffnell nodded. ''Course it was,' he said with his mouth full. 'And like the murder of Caterina Jacinto, if you come to that. Interrogation followed by disposal. But whoever did it has still got some unanswered questions. Presumably Bernardo's got the answers.'

'Bernardo's not a pro,' Bergerac said thoughtfully. 'So how – ?'

Tuffnell beamed at him. 'Plain as the nose on your face. It has to be something that happened in prison, doesn't it?'

'Could be.'

'It's the only time in his life that Bernardo is known to have mixed with that sort of crowd.' Tuffnell stuffed the remains of the last sandwich into his mouth. 'Worth enquiring, I thought. So I went down to the Scrubs and had a word with an assistant governor and a few warders. Jacinto spent some time as an orderly in the prison hospital. And while he was there he made a friend. Guess who? Brian Yellowthorn.'

'The man who was done for the bullion robbery?' Bergerac whistled. 'He's dead, isn't he?'

'Double pneumonia,' Tuffnell said with obvious satisfaction. 'Serve him right. He never showed any remorse for killing that security guard.'

'The bullion was never recovered,' Bergerac said. 'Six million quid, was it?'

'One night,' Tuffnell said dreamily, 'Yellowthorn thought he was dying. Jacinto talked to him for hours, apparently. I don't know what happened or what was said. But Yellowthorn cheered up and didn't die for another week or two. And a little message leaked out of the hospital and went round the Scrubs: *Jacinto's a mate of Brian's, so be nice to him.*'

Bergerac studied his untouched orange squash. He could see how Tuffnell's mind was working. As theories went, it was fine; but there was no proof. On the other hand, any theory was better than none at all.

'Who was behind the bullion robbery?' he asked. 'Someone must have funded it.'

'The Costain gang,' Tuffnell said placidly. 'That's the current thinking.'

Bergerac's lips tightened. A year or two earlier, he had been involved in the Costain case himself. The gang's leader, Mary Lou Costain, had killed one of his informers. She was dead herself now, and the world was no poorer for her passing.

'Most of them are inside,' Tuffnell continued. 'But there was one woman we missed. Worse than Costain herself, by all accounts. We couldn't pin a thing on her. Hasn't got a record, as far as we know. We're not even sure what she looks like or what her full name is. Specialized in contract kidnapping, they say, but open to suggestions.' He paused to empty his second pint. 'They used to call her Marilyn.'

Bergerac left New Scotland Yard shortly after three o'clock. Pale December sunshine filtered through a gap in the clouds. He decided to walk to Green Park, the nearest tube station on the Piccadilly line which would take him directly back to Heathrow.

To his surprise Tuffnell offered to come with him.

'It's a nice walk across the parks,' the old man said. The

pints he had consumed at lunchtime appeared to have had no effect on him whatsoever. 'Besides, I need to do some shopping. Bloody Christmas.'

Bergerac tried to suppress the memory of his own Christmas shopping. He cast around for a change of subject.

'My DCI sends his regards. Barney Crozier. He said he met you on a course at Hendon.'

'Crozier?' Tuffnell led the way into St James's Park. They walked along the shore of the lake. 'I remember. Sort of milk-and-water version of Bill Overstone.'

Bergerac grinned. 'He thought he saw someone else from the course – on Jersey, just the other day. Bloke named Ronny Quine.'

Tuffnell stopped abruptly. He looked up at Bergerac. His face was a mass of pouches and wrinkles.

'Quine left the force a few years back.'

Something in his voice alerted Bergerac. He looked enquiringly at Tuffnell.

'A rotten apple,' the old man said. 'Last I heard of him, he'd set up as a private detective.'

They walked on in silence. Tuffnell set a brisk pace. They crossed the Mall and entered Queen's Walk.

'I never liked that bloke,' he said suddenly. 'Tell you one thing: if he's on your island, I'd try and persuade him he'd be happier somewhere else.'

CHAPTER
13

Diamanté Lil was in a private room at the General Hospital.

She was reading a magazine and chewing her way through a substantial bunch of grapes when Susan arrived, laden with a carrier bag.

She looked up as the door opened, her face brightening. 'Bless you, Susan. You've no idea how bored I've been.'

Susan bent and kissed her. 'How are you?'

'All being well, I can go home tomorrow morning. It's stupid, really – I feel fine and there's a million and one things I need to do. But the doctor keeps pulling a long face and saying they like to be absolutely sure with head injuries. You know you're getting old when even the doctor looks young enough to be your daughter.'

Susan glanced round the room. The bedside locker and the windowsill were already crowded with cards and what looked like the contents of a small florist's shop.

'I see you've had a few visitors already.' She rummaged in her carrier bag and produced a box of chocolates. 'These are for you. I hope you haven't been swamped with them.'

'No one else has had the sense to bring chocolates,' Lil grinned. 'Most of the flowers are from Charlie Hungerford. I think he's got commercial designs on me. Is Jim back yet?'

'Not that I know of.' Susan sat down in the armchair with a sigh of relief. 'We're having dinner at his place tonight. He'd better get back in time.'

'Jim's cooking?'

Susan nodded.

'Ah, well,' Lil said comfortingly. 'Bit of a mixed blessing, if you ask me, but I suppose it's the thought that counts. Have a chocolate.' She leant back against the pillows and drew the bedjacket around her. 'You look as if you need a bit of pampering yourself. Maybe we should change places.'

'I'd better not have a chocolate – it'll spoil dinner.' Susan smothered a yawn. 'But you're right: I'm shattered. It's been a rough day. But we shouldn't be talking about me.'

'Why ever not?' Lil forced a smile. 'It takes my mind off my problems.'

'This business really worries you, doesn't it?' Susan squeezed Lil's hand. 'It's not just the bash on the head.'

Lil returned the pressure. 'I'm getting old,' she said with mock-solemnity. 'I know everyone thinks I'm armour-plated, but sometimes I feel as vulnerable as anyone else.' She made a determined effort to change the subject: 'And, talking about feelings, I've got a feeling that Alvaro is tied up with this: and that worries me. He's got about as much armour plating as the average rabbit.'

'Jim'll sort it out,' Susan said, with a conviction she didn't feel. 'And you'll feel better after a good night's sleep.'

The door opened and another visitor was ushered in. Susan withdrew her hand from Lil's. There would be no more time for confidences. Wearily she marshalled her social skills to greet the intruder.

'Lil, darling,' Deborah Hungerford said. 'You poor thing. Dad told me all about it.' She caught sight of Susan and the smile slipped away from her face. 'I hope I'm not interrupting.'

Susan stood up. 'I was just going.'

She had never admitted, even to Jim, her real feelings about Deborah Hungerford. It was more than a sort of post-dated jealousy, though that played a part in it; Jim would never be entirely free of Deborah, and both of them knew it.

The situation might have been tolerable if Deborah had been a different sort of person. But she was always well-dressed, well-groomed and insufferably self-confident. In her presence, Susan became clumsy, at least in her own eyes. Even now she was uneasily conscious that she should have repaired her make-up before leaving the office, that there was a mark on her skirt and that a hard day's work had left her ill-equipped to deal on equal terms with wealthy women of leisure.

'Please don't go for my sake,' Deborah said in her best lady-of-the-manor voice.

Susan picked up the carrier bag. One of the handles gave way. A tin of baked beans rolled slowly across the floor. Jim had a childish taste for baked beans in tomato sauce.

Deborah stared at the tin as if she had never seen a baked bean in her life. It came to rest against the toe of a high-heeled shoe which had probably cost more than Susan earned in a week. Deborah bent gracefully and picked it up.

'Carrier bags are so tiresome,' she said as she handed it back. 'Always breaking at the wrong moment.'

Susan flushed and mumbled her thanks.

Lil came to her rescue with a long anecdote from her distant youth in Swinging London, about the time she had been humiliated in Harrods' Food Hall when a carrier bag disintegrated in her hand.

'. . . About a week's dirty washing was on display. I was just on my way to the launderette. But there was this terribly nice young Arab who helped me pick it all up. And, do you know, he *bought* me a bag to put it in . . .'

Susan moved towards the door.

'Oh, I wanted to thank you,' Deborah said. 'You've been

so helpful about Kim's party. I do hope it isn't a bore for you.'

Her expression added a subtext: *I don't like you barging into my daughter's life.*

Susan let herself into Bergerac's flat. A bath and a change of clothes improved her mood considerably.

It surprised her that Jim wasn't back yet. She wondered whether to ring the Bureau – he must have returned from London by now. But she disliked phoning him at the office: it savoured of the nagging wife; and besides, she knew that Barney Crozier disapproved of personal calls.

At eight o'clock she decided that she might as well start cooking dinner; if she waited for Jim – who was in any case the world's slowest cook – they probably wouldn't eat until midnight.

She put a tape in the music centre and set to work. First the rice. Then a quick check in the fridge which showed her that, yet again, Jim had forgotten to buy the salad vegetables. They would just have to make do with two overripe tomatoes, half an elderly avocado and a handful of lettuce leaves turning brown at the edges.

Just as she had finished the curry sauce that was to go over the chicken breasts, she heard his key turning in the lock. *Typical*, she thought; *Jim has a great sense of timing.* It was one of those characteristics that worked both ways.

He burst into the living room, flinging his briefcase on the sofa with one hand and tugging off his tie with the other. Then he caught sight of her and an expression of almost comical dismay crossed his face.

'Oh, no – I completely forgot about tonight.' He sniffed the air appreciatively. 'And I'm meant to be cooking you a meal.'

'It doesn't matter,' Susan said untruthfully.

He kissed her absent-mindedly on the cheek. 'I'll make

up for it, I promise. I'm afraid I've got to go out again. I just came back for a jersey and another jacket.'

'But I thought you said – '

'I know, I'm meant to be off duty. But I've got to relieve Barry Goddard.' He disappeared into the bedroom and opened the wardrobe. 'Surveillance job – he's spent most of today sitting in a car. I'd send someone else but half the Bureau seems to be down with flu.'

She said nothing, which wasn't easy. She wasn't even Jim's wife. Mistresses don't have many rights. In any case they had a tacit agreement to respect the demands made by each other's jobs. He had told her long ago that one of the main reasons for the break-up of his marriage to Deborah was her inability to accept the long, unsocial and unpredictable hours a policeman had to work.

'Did you manage to see Lil?' Jim's voice was muffled by the jersey he was tugging over his head. 'I didn't have time myself.'

'Yes.' Susan switched off the tape and sat down on the sofa. 'On my way back from work.'

'How is she?'

'Mending physically, but rather in the doldrums emotionally.'

Just like me, she added silently to herself.

Aloud she said: 'Do you want something to eat? The chicken's nearly ready. Or there's baked beans.'

'No time, I'm afraid. I'll get a takeaway or something.'

That meant he wouldn't eat anything. She shrugged. Why should she care? Feeding him was none of her business.

Jim emerged from the bedroom, pulling on a heavy reefer jacket.

'I don't know when I'll be back,' he said. 'Are you staying?'

She thought briefly of the ruined dinner. Jim could be

out all night. If she stayed here she would be alone with a sabotaged evening. It was not the most enticing of prospects.

She shook her head. 'I'll go back home, I think.'

'I'm sorry about this, love.' He kissed the top of her head. 'I'll call you tomorrow morning.'

The door slammed behind him. Susan remained where she was for a long moment. Then she stood up and walked slowly into the kitchen. Jim kept a bottle of Scotch for her in the cupboard under the window. She poured herself the equivalent of two pub doubles and added ice. As she sipped it, she stared bleakly at her reflection in the uncurtained windowpane.

The chicken smelled as if it were burning. What the hell.

'It's your turn to feed the babies,' Norma said. 'I did it last night.'

'I had other things to do,' Quine said. 'Remember?'

'That's different.' Norma lit a cigarette and lay back on one of the bunks. 'You'd better hurry up. Oliver'll be here in a moment.'

Ronny Quine recognized defeat when he saw it; since he and Norma Jean Veldman had gone into partnership, defeat had become increasingly familiar to him. It wasn't worth arguing with Norma.

He went into the tiny galley and lit one of the Calor gas rings. He took a couple of tins at random. Oxtail soup in one, and spaghetti in the other. Last night's saucepan stood on the draining board; a thin layer of Irish stew had congealed on the bottom. No point in washing it up now, he thought – it would only need doing again afterwards. He opened the tins and spooned their contents into the pan.

'That looks disgusting,' Norma said through the open door.

Quine shrugged. 'We're not eating it. Where's the bread?'

'In the bread-bin, dummy.'

He hacked off a couple of doorsteps from the loaf. By the time he had finished, the unsavoury mess on the stove was beginning to bubble.

'It stinks,' Norma said. 'You turned up the gas too high.'

'It's your fault. You should have washed the saucepan. It's the remains of the stew that's burning.'

Quine scraped the base of the saucepan with a spoon. The smell of burning grew worse. Norma cocked her head.

'Here's wonder-boy,' she said. 'Dead on time.'

Oliver burst into the saloon. 'All set?'

'Grub's up,' Quine said. He put a lid on the saucepan and thrust the bread and a couple of spoons into a carrier bag.

'Smells awful,' Oliver said.

'Don't you start. What do you want? Gourmet bloody cooking?'

Quine opened a locker above the starboard bunk and took out the automatic. He checked the action. Oliver's eyes strayed to Norma on the other bunk. She gave him a lazy smile.

'Is all this really necessary?' Oliver said suddenly. 'Two of us going, I mean. You could manage by yourself, couldn't you, Ronny? You've got the gun.'

'No way.' Quine slipped the gun in his pocket. 'Always two of us – we agreed.'

'But it's not as if they could do anything.'

Quine knew how Oliver's mind was working. The fat bastard couldn't keep his eyes off Norma when they were in the same room. Well, tough. Quine wasn't going to play gooseberry for Oliver's sake.

'We made the rules,' he said. 'And we stick to them.

There's no sense in taking risks.' He glanced at Norma. 'Right, sweetheart?'

For a moment he thought she wasn't going to back him up. Then she nodded.

'Ronny's got a point, you know,' she told Oliver. 'If you don't take chances, you don't get hurt.'

'Oh, all right.' Oliver's lower lip protruded; it made him look like a child on the verge of tears. 'Well, come on, Ronny. Let's get it over with.'

Charlie Hungerford was lonely.

Deborah had taken Kim out to see some friends in St Helier. He had dinner by himself in the huge dining room. He ate by candlelight because it was the sort of thing they did in old films about upper-crust life.

As usual he sat at the head of the table. In front of him the polished mahogany stretched away into the shadows at the far end of the room. Puddles of reflected candlelight emphasized its bare surface. Ranged round the table were empty chairs, like a line of mute, unwanted guests.

Halfway through the meal he could stand it no longer. He flicked down the switch by the door, flooding the room with the harsh glare of electric light. If anything it made things worse. The Christmas decorations mocked him. A Georgian manor was all very well, but it needed people to complement the furniture and fittings. Otherwise it felt just like a barracks after the troops had pulled out.

Normally, he avoided solitude. It was one reason why he liked Deborah to live at home, why he cultivated a wide circle of friends and why he pursued so assiduously his range of business and political interests. But occasionally there were yawning gaps in his diary. When he peered through the gaps he was frightened by what he saw.

He picked at the pudding his cook had left him, but pushed the plate away after a few mouthfuls. Nothing was arranged for this evening and nothing for tomorrow. Even the grandfather clock in the corner had more to do than he did.

The cheeseboard was waiting for him. But he didn't need cheese. He needed a treat, something to cheer him up.

He pushed back his chair and collected the decanter of brandy from the sideboard. The fire was still burning in the library. He poked it into a blaze and tossed on two more logs. Brandy in one hand, cigar in the other, he opened the pseudo-Chippendale cabinet beneath the video.

Here they were – shelf after shelf of home movies. The early ones had originally been on ciné film, but Hungerford had had them transferred to video. They recorded for posterity the biggest parties and the greatest triumphs of Hungerford's career. They provided persuasive answers to the awkward questions raised by the gaps in his diary. He pulled on his cigar and ran his eyes along the spines of the tapes.

Not one of the early ones, perhaps. At present he had no wish to be reminded of his life in Yorkshire; besides, his dead wife featured prominently in many of them and he preferred not to think about her.

He hesitated for a moment over the tape which recorded Deborah's wedding to Jim Bergerac. Good God – how time passed: the wedding was nearer twenty years ago than ten. Now that had been a real bash. Two or three hundred guests and champagne by the bucketful – and none of your non-vintage rubbish, either. Deborah had looked stunning, he remembered – and so she should have: the dress had cost a mint; but it had cleverly concealed the fact that she was already pregnant.

No – not the wedding. It would mean watching Jim Bergerac prancing around in morning dress – and listening once more to that snide speech of his, which had raised more laughs than Charlie's had.

He moved on to happier occasions. He narrowed the shortlist down to two: his Gala Garden Party last year, which had an especially fine sequence of himself and the Lieutenant-Governor inspecting the grounds; or the opening ceremony of the new classroom block at the primary school, when Charlie had helped the Bailiff of Jersey to unveil the commemorative plaque (*The Charles Hungerford Wing was erected through the generosity of . . .*).

Then the phone rang. Hungerford forgot about the past and made a dash for it. Maybe his future was calling.

'Charlie? This is Guy Pilsen-Smith. Not disturbing you, I hope?'

'No, no. I was just – '

'Look, would you and Deborah be free for dinner tomorrow? I know it's short notice, but I didn't know myself till this evening. I was having a drink at the Yacht Club, and one thing led to another. You know how it is. Can you manage it by any chance?'

'Well, let me see.' Hungerford pretended to consider his busy social schedule. 'If I do a little – er – re-arranging, I think I might be – '

'Good,' Pilsen-Smith cut in. 'By the way, I've got the Attorney-General coming, and a couple of your colleagues on the Law and Order Committee.'

'Oh, really?'

'Black tie, of course. Seven-thirty for eight suit you? Good. 'Bye now, Charlie.'

CHAPTER
14

The English had a proverb for it: *Tread on a worm and it will turn.*

He had made his plan long ago. His preparations were complete. That was the easy part. The difficult part was waiting.

The view from the study window showed him the full frontage of Carlton House. Directly opposite, but a storey higher, was the window of his former room. His position commanded both the front door and the passage which ran round the house to the side door and then on to the backyard.

All day he had watched the comings and goings below him. From the first, however, he had thought it more likely that they would wait for darkness before they came. After all, they were creatures of the night. He was sure they would approach from the front; access to the back of the house was blocked by the gas-works.

Fragments of prayers, half-remembered and half-understood, chased through his mind as he crouched by the window. Sometimes he muttered them aloud. He had no conscious intention of praying, but the jumble of Latin syllables had a calming effect on him. It drew him back to the old ways – to his mother on her knees; to the dim but terrifying memory of his grandfather, old Eusebio Ferreira, confronting God on equal terms in the little whitewashed church on the side of the mountain.

He was tempted to have a drink – not once but often;

and sometimes the temptation was all but unbearable. But a clear head and a steady hand were essential. Afterwards, he promised himself, he would drink his fill; he would drink the Colonel's whisky until he passed out. Then the police could do what they liked with him. It would no longer matter.

There was another, more insidious, temptation. The telephone was still connected. He could phone Lil's Place and talk to Madame. She was a good woman and perhaps she would help him to escape from this dreadful island. He yearned for the sympathy she could give him. There had been no woman in his life since Caterina died.

But that would be the way of the coward. Madame would be sympathetic, yes; but sooner or later she would hand him over to her policeman friend; she had her loyalties too. It would all be over: he would be damned for ever – not just in the world's eyes but in his own. No, he had set his trap and now he must spring it on his enemies.

There was another English proverb he recalled: *As well be hanged for a sheep as a lamb.*

Bergerac opened the passenger door and nodded to the young DC.

'Hop it, Ben. It's way past your bedtime.'

'Thanks, Sarge.'

The detective constable scrambled out of the car and trotted off in the direction of the Bureau. It was too cold to walk and he was probably afraid that Bergerac might change his mind.

Bergerac climbed into the car and closed the door. In the driver's seat, Goddard was scowling through the windscreen.

'You're late,' he said without turning his head.

'I'm sorry, Barry.' It occurred to Bergerac that he was apologizing to everyone this evening. 'Anything to report?'

'Nothing. Mrs Le Davre did her shopping. One or two men came out and in – lodgers, I presume; none of them looked like your mystery man. No sign of your waiter, either.'

'You've not just sat here all day, have you?'

Goddard shook his head. 'Hourly checks on foot, just like you said. The approach at the back is blocked by the gas-works. If anyone comes, it'll be from this side. One of the neighbours is the curious type. I saw a curtain moving twice as I walked by.'

Bergerac groaned. Curious neighbours had their uses; but they were a definite liability for surveillance work.

'Which house?' he asked.

'The one directly opposite. You can't see it from here.'

'Isn't that where Colonel Hebben lives? I thought it was empty at this time of year.'

Goddard shrugged. 'Maybe he let it. People do.'

'Barry – do me a favour. When you get back to the Bureau, just check it out, will you? And call me back on the R/T.'

'Oh, come on, Jim – I've got a date. Have a heart – I'm half an hour overdue already.'

'I had a date too,' Bergerac said. 'And as a matter of fact I went off duty officially about three hours ago. Just do it, OK?'

'I always said this was a cock-eyed scheme,' Goddard muttered.

'I don't care what you said. There's another thing I want you to do. Chase up Giles and send him over here. He's meant to be on the graveyard shift. You'll probably have to leave a message for him.'

'Why isn't he here now, then? At least two officers at any one time on a surveillance job: that's what it says in the Regulations.'

Bergerac sighed. Goddard was a good officer – very good

if the truth be told — but he had an awkward streak which came out when he felt he was unfairly under pressure. In times of stress the barrack-room lawyer emerged from some corner of his personality. In the old days Bergerac himself had been like that. Sometimes — when Crozier was exceptionally unbearable — he still was.

'Listen,' he said, more gently than before. 'We're under-staffed as it is. Then we've got pre-Christmas leave to deal with, plus an outbreak of flu. It's tough on all of us, OK?'

'Yes, but — '

Bergerac overrode the interruption: 'And if you want to go by the book, this is how we play it. Giles is out on a case, and he's unlikely to be back before midnight. If you're so damned keen on the Regulations you wait here with me till he turns up. *At least two officers at any one time*' — he mimicked Goddard's tone — 'for God's sake, Barry! Can't you see I'm trying to do you a favour?'

The silence which followed was broken only by the sound of Goddard's fingernail scratching the cover of the steering wheel.

'Sorry,' he said at last. 'I lost my rag. It's been a long day.'

For a moment neither of them said anything. They stared down the empty street. At this time of night there was little traffic. The wind drove a crumpled sheet of newspaper from one side of the road to the other. It was very cold in the car and even worse outside. Maybe Goddard was right: this was a cock-eyed scheme.

Bergerac stirred. 'It's going to be a long night, too.'

Norma Jean was driving. The 20 m.p.h. speed limit in built-up areas irked her enormously. What was the use of a powerful car if you could hardly get above second gear?

They came into St Helier by Queen's Road. Quine was map-reading by the light of a small torch.

'Left at the traffic lights,' he said. 'And at the next lights we want to go right.'

'I don't want to park too close,' Norma said. She pulled over to allow a police car to pass. 'Charming. They might have said thank you.'

'Police headquarters is just down there,' Quine told her.

'You're a mine of useless information, Ronny.'

The second set of lights was green.

'Where now?' she asked.

'Just carry on. We'll come to a cinema on the right. There's a car park behind it – we could try that. Or maybe somewhere on the street. What worries me is afterwards.'

'Leave it to Auntie Norma.'

'Well, what are we going to do?'

'We'll find a door or a window. That won't be a problem, not with your specialized skills. For God's sake, it's only a two-bit boarding-house by all accounts. We've got his room number. So once we're inside, we just go and find him.'

'And then?'

In the darkness she drew back her lips in a smile. 'You can leave it all to me, Ronny. That's my speciality.'

'Colonel and Mrs Hebben are in Majorca,' Goddard said against a background of static. 'According to this, they aren't coming back till April. They never let the house. Over.'

'Keys?' Bergerac said. 'Over.'

'Mrs Le Davre, Carlton House, Oxford Road.' Goddard hesitated. 'It says here that she airs the house once a week. Over.'

'Could it have been her you saw? Over.'

'No way. The second time was just after she'd come back from the market. I'd've seen her if she'd crossed the road. Over.'

'You'd better get back here – '

'But Jim, Giles is – '

'I don't want Giles later,' Bergerac said. 'I want you now. Over and out.'

Just after midnight he caught his first sight of them.

First he heard them. Despite the cold he had opened the study window – not enough to be visible from outside; but sufficiently to hear sounds from the street.

They were walking northwards. The woman's high heels clicked on the pavement, clearly audible in the relative quiet of a winter night in St Helier. Jacinto tensed himself – as he had done so often before in his long vigil. He held his breath as they came within his range of vision.

He was almost fooled – they looked such a respectable couple, so unlike the animals he remembered. The man wore a raglan overcoat and his shoes gleamed as they passed a street lamp. The woman had some kind of fur and a long dress beneath. A headscarf covered her hair. They walked slowly – lingering like lovers, unwilling for their evening to end.

But it was too cold for lovers to linger outside. And people with expensive clothes had expensive cars to go with them.

They did not pause outside Carlton House, though Jacinto thought their pace slowed momentarily. The man murmured something and the woman laughed softly. Soon they were out of sight again.

A reconnaissance, perhaps? On the other hand, he had not seen their faces clearly; and the coat and the fur masked their shapes so it was possible he was mistaken. After all he had only seen them together once before, and in very different circumstances.

The click of the high heels diminished in volume. He strained to follow them with his ears. The clicks became fainter and fainter until they were indistinguishable from the distant roar of traffic and the moaning of the wind.

His doubts multiplied. Love made nonsense of normal behaviour. Maybe they were precisely what they seemed. He did not even know for certain that Ronny and the woman would come back to look for him here. Maybe he was a fool who would do better to turn the Colonel's revolver on himself.

Goddard was in a foul temper when he reached the car, but Bergerac gave him no time to vent his anger.

'Good lad,' he said briskly. 'You stay here. I want to have a look at that house.'

'You going to get the keys from Mrs Le Davre?'

Bergerac shook his head. 'Might have to, later. But right now it's softly, softly. There's an alley for tradesmen along the back of the houses on that side of the road.'

'Crozier's not going to like this,' Goddard said.

His resentment dropped away from him. Jim Bergerac could be a real slave-driver, but at least he wasn't as hidebound as most officers on his level and above.

'Can't say I think it's a bundle of fun myself.' Bergerac reached for the door handle. 'By the way a man and a woman came past, a few minutes ago. Well-dressed, early middle-age. I couldn't get a good look at them, but they seemed very – what's the word? – affectionate.'

'So?'

'Bit cold for courting al fresco, isn't it?'

'Did they show any interest in Carlton House?'

'Afraid not. But you never know. Keep your eyes open and don't let them see the car's occupied if they do turn up again.'

Bergerac opened the door and slid out of the car. Goddard hunched himself down in the seat and tried to imagine what it was like to be warm.

He thought briefly of what his girlfriend had said when he phoned from the Bureau to cancel their all-night date. The memory was depressing. It was a pity, but perhaps best in the long run that they had to end this way. If she couldn't accept that the job had to come first, nine times out of ten, the relationship would never have worked in the long term. Better for both of them to find out sooner rather than later.

A cat ran across the road and dived through a wrought-iron gate two doors down from Carlton House. Nothing else was moving.

But behind him — faint but growing steadily louder — came the sound of footsteps. They tapped daintily along the pavement.

Far away, he heard the click of high-heeled shoes. The clicks grew louder as the shoes drew closer.

Now . . .

He gasped greedily for air. The gun seemed to double in weight. His hands were slippery with oil and sweat.

The study door was open. He was at the head of the stairs. It seemed to him that he floated, rather than ran, down to the hall. There was no time to think and no time to change direction.

Part of his mind was separate from all this — it might have belonged to someone else. It threw up an image, which he registered without wishing to understand: a brightly coloured toy train ran for ever round a circular track; there was nowhere else for it to go. Once his cousin Jorge had owned such a train, and Bernardo had lusted after it.

His eyes had long since accustomed themselves to the semi-darkness. The black-and-white tiles in the hall shimmered before him. He tripped over the edge of a rug and fell against the front door.

The bolts were already undone. He had found a key for the mortice lock. Only the Yale remained.

He twisted the knob and pulled. The door swung back.

There they were on the other side of the street. He opened his mouth.

Behind him – somewhere in the depths of the house – came the chink of metal on stone.

CHAPTER
15

'No! No! For Christ's sake!'

The words were barely above the level of a whisper. But they were perfectly audible on the other side of the road. So was the anguish in Jacinto's voice.

Norma Jean spun round; her dress swirled round her ankles. Quine's reactions were a split second slower than hers. The house opposite had iron railings and a short flight of steps leading up to the front door. Framed in the doorway was a white, contorted face.

'It's him.' She gripped Quine's arm. 'Go!'

It was as though she had sicked on a dog. Quine loped across the street; despite his bulk he had a surprising turn of speed. Jacinto was no longer in the doorway. The door swung shut with a thud.

She glanced quickly up and down the road. Nothing was stirring. She followed Quine, walking quickly but without haste. Ronny pushed against the door and it opened noiselessly; the stupid little dago must have left it on the latch. He vanished inside.

It was much darker in the house than outside. The door, which was on a spring, closed of its own accord; she did not notice that Jacinto had left it on the latch, for her mind was on other things.

She realized immediately that there was no need to hurry: the house smelled cold and untenanted; and Ronny knew his job. It was better to move slowly and surely. She had time to savour this experience. Someone was thundering up a flight of stairs – presumably Ronny in hot pursuit of Jacinto. She fumbled in her handbag.

Her fingers closed round a torch. She switched it on and advanced slowly to the foot of the stairs. Its thin beam picked out the treads, one by one. As the light rose upwards, so did her excitement. Very soon, Jacinto would have to talk. She wanted to hear what he had to say, naturally; but she would also enjoy making him say it.

The darkness at the head of the stairs gave way to a wavering light – dim and patchy, as if the source was in a neighbouring room rather than on the landing itself. Someone else must have a torch. She heard the murmur of voices above her head; they were pitched too low for her to distinguish the words or even the speakers.

Suddenly Ronny Quine raised his voice: 'No, Bernardo. Please. Look, chum, let's not get over-excited. No! *Please!*'

Some sort of trap – ?

Alarm was only part of her reaction; the excitement intensified too. Jacinto had no friends: he must be alone. It was always more interesting when you had a challenge to deal with.

The light on the landing disappeared as abruptly as it had come. The voices, quieter now, mumbled above her head. Norma Jean licked her lips. She took the knife from her handbag. Its thin blade glinted in the light of the torch.

'You'd better let me have that,' a man said in the darkness behind her. 'You might cut someone.'

This time she felt only alarm. *Freelance or copper?*

Whoever he was, he was fast and quiet. The words were still in the air and she had hardly begun to turn when the hand clamped itself round her right wrist. A second hand joined the first. The hands twisted. She shrieked. The knife fell; it thudded on the stair carpet, bounced away and tinkled on the tiles of the hall.

But she still had the torch. She thrust it upwards aiming

blindly for the vulnerable spot where the neck joins the chin. A grunt of pain rewarded her. The torch went out.

The grip on her arm slackened. She stamped downwards with her two-inch heel; simultaneously she drove her left elbow behind her; each blow gained impetus from the other.

The heel jarred uselessly against the tiles but the elbow struck lucky. This time her attacker shouted with pain.

The knife – she needed the knife to finish the job.

The stranger was retching now. He sounded only a yard or two away. She thumbed the button on the torch but nothing happened. The bloody bulb must have gone. The streetlight filtered weakly through the fanlight above the door. Her assailant was a blurred shadow.

'Why don't you put that down, Bernardo?' Quine said quickly, somewhere above her head; there was an edge of panic in his voice. 'Tell you what, let's have a drink and talk this over. Man to man, like.'

He must have heard, she thought; why wasn't he down here helping? It was all happening too fast. *A trap?*

She lifted the hem of her skirt and kicked upwards with all the force she could muster. The point of her shoe connected with the shadow. He screamed again, more loudly than before. *That's the way to treat a man – hit him where it hurts.*

The front door opened.

Her triumph evaporated instantly. She stifled the scream that rose in her throat. A man was standing in the doorway. The light from a powerful torch burst into the hall, illuminating her groaning victim on the floor. The interruption seemed to give him strength. He hauled himself on to his hands and knees.

'Upstairs, Barry.' The voice was faint and strained but the authority in it was unmistakable. 'Leave this one to me.'

Through the open door she heard the wail of a distant police siren.

The odds were lengthening. It was time to go. The torchlight glittered on a strip of metal at the foot of the stairs.

Norma Jean scooped up the knife and darted into the passage which led to the rear of the house. The new arrival thundered up the stairs. The other man was on his feet again. She burst through a door and cannoned into a table. A fridge-freezer gleamed in one corner. The kitchen. But where was the back door?

The man was after her. His breathing came in ragged gasps. She felt a brief and unwilling admiration for his obstinacy.

Dear God! The back door was ajar. No need to use the knife on him after all – not yet.

Outside, she found herself in a covered passageway. One end gave on to the small garden; the other was blocked by a gate she remembered seeing from the road. She made a dash for the gate.

The man was close behind her now. She fumbled for the latch with her left hand. The gate opened. She had no choice. He was too close. She would have to use the knife.

Then she heard a shot.

It was muffled by the walls of the house, but still loud in the confined space of the passage.

Her pursuer stopped, leaning against one wall for support. Norma Jean slammed the gate behind her.

The siren sounded much louder in the street. She turned right, away from the police car. Holding up her skirt, she ran as fast as high heels would allow her. Once round the corner, she stopped and snatched off both shoes. She could make much better speed in stockinged feet. One shoe slipped from her hand and skidded into the gutter. The police car was now in the upper end of Oxford Road.

Norma Jean ran on.

Goddard plunged up the stairs.

Below him the hall was in confusion. The woman looked like a huge bear in that coat. But it had not occurred to him to question Bergerac's order. Jim knew what he was doing.

On the landing he paused to get his bearings. Torchlight was visible around one partly opened door. He advanced cautiously towards it.

'Stay in that chair, Ronny.' The soft, stumbling voice was Jacinto's. 'Or you're a dead man, I tell you.'

'Sure. Bernardo. Anything you say. You want a little drink?'

The second man had a London accent, hoarse to begin with and now strained as well.

'You killed Caterina. Then you make the police think I did it. I cannot forgive.'

'It was an accident. Besides, it wasn't me who actually – '

'You were there. You could have stopped it.'

'Let me tell you about it. It's not what you think. You see, what happened – '

'You try to keep me talking till your woman comes?' Jacinto must have moved, for a floorboard creaked. 'Now you are between me and the door. You are in the middle, Ronny. Remember that.'

The police siren was clearly audible now.

Then it was drowned by the shot.

Goddard just prevented himself from rushing into the room.

'Bernardo . . .' The voice was reduced to a whisper but at least it meant that Ronny was still alive.

'I told you not to move.'

145

The stench of cordite drifted on to the landing.

'I'll talk to the police,' Ronny said. 'I'll tell them everything, I swear it. You'll be cleared.'

'I don't want to be cleared, not now. You owe me blood, Ronny. That's what I want. I'm going to kill you.'

Goddard believed him. Time had run out for all three of them. He tapped politely on the door and pushed it open.

'Police,' he said, as calmly as he could, waiting for the bullet to hit him. He held his hands up to show that he was unarmed. Somehow he had to lower the emotional temperature. 'Bureau des Etrangers. You want to see my warrant card, Mr Jacinto?'

A torch was propped up on the mantelpiece; the mirror above increased the light it gave. Two big armchairs had their backs to the door. Above one of them, Ronny's head and shoulders were visible. He did not look round. *Jim's mystery man?*

Jacinto crouched beyond the chair, his back against the wall; he was holding a heavy service revolver in both hands. Goddard could see little of his face except the whites of his eyes.

'No,' Jacinto said. 'Oh, God, I don't want to kill *you*.'

'Here,' Goddard murmured as though Jacinto was a fractious child. 'Let me show you my warrant card.'

His right hand moved slowly towards the inside pocket of his jacket.

'Stop!'

The gun jerked upwards from Ronny. Goddard stopped moving.

'This man and his woman killed my wife,' Jacinto said. 'So I kill him. OK?'

'Leave him to us, Bernardo,' Goddard said softly. 'We know what he's done. We'll deal with him, I promise.'

The gun wavered in Jacinto's hands. The muzzle moved back to cover Ronny. The big man covered his face with his hands. Jacinto's finger tightened on the trigger.

146

'It won't solve anything,' Goddard said. 'Put the gun down. Leave him to us.'

He calculated positions and distances. A sudden rush was out of the question. There were too many obstacles in the way. *Keep him talking.*

'Why did they kill Caterina, Bernardo?'

The little man scrambled to his feet. The gun was still pointing at Ronny but now he was looking at Goddard. 'They were trying to make her talk. They wanted her to tell them things she did not know.'

'What things?'

'Something I knew.'

'Then why weren't they asking you?'

Jacinto swallowed. 'I was too drunk to speak. She died because of me, you know? It was my fault too.'

'No,' Goddard said. 'It was not your fault. You didn't kill her. Tell me what happened.'

Where the hell is that patrol car?

'They broke into our flat that night.' Jacinto was weeping now; Goddard had to strain to hear what he was saying. 'I couldn't move, I couldn't do anything except watch. They thought I was asleep.'

The tears prevented him from continuing.

'Go on,' Goddard said. 'You can tell me.'

'They did things to Caterina with a knife.' The gun drooped; its muzzle was now resting on the carpet. Jacinto wiped his eyes with the back of one hand. 'The . . . the neighbours banged on the wall. This man was worried. He made the woman go with him. And then I – '

There were soft footsteps on the stairs, pausing between each tread. *Pray God it's Jim, not the woman.*

Without warning, Ronny pulled himself to his feet. His face was working with panic. Goddard swore aloud. The room was a blur of movement and yet everything seemed to happen very slowly.

Jacinto raised the gun. Ronny leapt sideways; both feet left the floor. For a split second he looked like an ungainly ballet dancer. One foot hit the ground. The other snagged against the side of another armchair. The heavy body swung round in an arc. Ronny tried to save himself by grabbing the back of a chair. His hand closed round emptiness. His head smashed into the corner of an oak bureau. He lay, unmoving, in an untidy huddle on the carpet. A trickle of blood oozed from above his ear.

At the same moment the police car arrived. The siren died. Flashes of cold blue light came through the uncurtained window like a series of electric shocks.

Jacinto stood over the fallen man. He raised the gun.

'Bernardo,' Goddard said, 'he's not worth it.'

A floorboard creaked behind him on the landing. He dared not turn to see who it was.

Jacinto slowly lowered the gun. His fingers relaxed their grip on the butt. The revolver fell to the floor. Goddard dived for it. He rolled as he landed. His hands closed round the barrel. The back of his body jolted into Jacinto.

Goddard scrambled to his feet, holding the gun away from him. Bergerac was standing in the doorway. Ronny lay where he had fallen, breathing heavily through his mouth.

Jacinto leant against the bureau. For the first time Goddard could see him properly. He was mud-stained, unshaven and seemingly unconscious of his surroundings.

'I cannot do it,' he said with a sob. He let go of the bureau and, hugging himself with both arms, swayed to and fro. 'I cannot kill him, Caterina. Even now I am a coward.'

CHAPTER
16

'This'll go down on your file, Sergeant,' Crozier said, 'make no mistake about that. An official reprimand, maybe.'

Bergerac, standing stiffly in front of the desk, bit back the savage answer he wanted to make.

'The operation wasn't a failure,' he pointed out.

It was a weak defence, but at present he couldn't do better. He had managed a couple of hours' sleep last night in his empty flat – if you could call it sleep. Susan's absence and the bungled arrests had prevented him from sinking below the level of a doze. He felt almost as though he had a hangover. Sometimes life could be bloody unfair.

'If it hadn't been for Goddard,' Crozier said, 'it would have been a total disaster. At least *he* had the sense to radio in before leaving the car.'

'I felt we had to be discreet,' Bergerac protested. 'There simply wasn't the manpower available.'

'You know the Regulations as well as I do.'

'Look, Barney – we got Jacinto: that's something, isn't it? And we've got Ronny Quine.'

'But he's not talking, is he?' Crozier scowled. 'Ex-coppers are the worst sort of prisoners: they know all the dodges.'

'We can get him for the murder of Mrs Jacinto. As an accessory, at least. Goddard heard him admit to it, and Jacinto was an eye-witness.'

'Jacinto's a drunk with a record. He had a gun in his hand when Quine talked. Can you imagine what a defence counsel would make of that? Besides, Jacinto isn't talking, either.'

'What?'

Crozier nodded. 'He wouldn't sign the statement he made last night.' His voice became a venomous parody of the little waiter's: 'He will only talk to Madame's policeman.'

Bergerac thought it diplomatic to change the subject. 'Any news about Quine's woman?'

'What woman?' Crozier sighed with exasperation. 'All we've got is a cheap Italian shoe – size six, black patent-leather, high-heeled, left foot. Goddard found it in Gas Place. We don't even know whose it is.'

'Just like Prince Charming,' Bergerac murmured.

Fortunately Crozier missed the interruption. 'Quine won't admit he was with a woman,' he went on. 'Not yet. That won't wash because both you and Goddard saw them together. But he won't say where he's been staying, either. I told you, Jim: he's not talking. He knows his rights.'

'Marilyn must be quite a woman,' Bergerac said.

'Eh?'

'Stands to reason, doesn't it? Quine would talk if he felt it was in his best interests. So it looks like he's more scared of her than he is of us. Or maybe he thinks she can get him out.'

Crozier shrugged. 'The way things are going, he won't need much help from her.' He picked up his phone and punched a number. 'I'll tell them we want Jacinto in an interrogation room. I just hope you have more success than I did.'

A few minutes later, the two men left the office. Bergerac knew that the threat of an official reprimand was more apparent than real; Crozier had been venting his frustration and Bergerac happened to get in the way. But Barney was badly rattled about this case – and that in itself was worrying. It meant that he must be under a lot of pressure from above.

Jacinto was waiting for them in one of the harshly lit interrogation rooms. He was smoking a cigarette, and someone had given him a cup of coffee in a plastic cup.

Crozier told the uniformed constable at the door to wait outside. 'Here's Madame's friend, Bernardo.' He spoke slowly as though to a retarded child. 'Now you can start talking, eh?'

Jacinto's eyes flicked from Crozier to Bergerac, and then down to the floor. His expression gave nothing away except his unhappiness.

'I told Lil you're safe,' Bergerac said. 'She's been worried about you. Did they tell you she was attacked?'

'What?' Jacinto's face was suddenly alive. 'Madame was attacked? Is she hurt? Who did it?'

'She's mending – she'll be out of hospital today, all being well. There was a break-in at the nightclub. We think Quine did it, but we can't prove it yet. He was probably looking for your address at the time.'

Jacinto buried his face in his hands. 'It is my fault. And Madame was so kind.'

'The best way you can help her is by telling us everything. That way we may be able to get Quine.'

The little man raised his face. Bergerac was shocked by the misery he saw.

'Did they tell you about my wife?' Jacinto said.

'We know all about that, Bernardo.'

'I didn't kill her, I swear it. It was the woman. But Quine was there. I was too drunk to stop them but I saw it happen. Oh, God – what that woman did with the knife – '

'I believe you.' Bergerac had seen Tuffnell's report on the subject; he didn't want to hear Jacinto's version now. 'I believe you,' he repeated, noticing the doubt on the little man's face. 'It's all right.'

Whether a jury would believe Jacinto was another matter.

'I wanted to kill them for her sake. So I laid a trap. But I couldn't do it. I was not strong enough.' He tapped his chest. 'Strong enough in the heart.'

'It's just as well,' Bergerac said. 'What you call revenge, we call murder. Tell us what they wanted.'

Jacinto glanced at Crozier, who was sensible enough not to be caught looking at the prisoner. He turned back to Bergerac.

'When I was in prison,' he said hesitantly, 'there was a man. A man who died.'

'Brian Yellowthorn?'

Jacinto nodded, relieved to find that he did not need to explain everything. He drew on his cigarette and stubbed it out in the tin that served as an ashtray.

'Did Yellowthorn talk to you?' Bergerac said.

'One night he did. It was in the hospital. I brought him water. He was thirsty but most of all he wanted to talk.' Jacinto shrugged. 'You see, he was very much afraid.'

'Afraid? Why?'

'Of death. Naturally. We are all afraid of death. He was a bad man, but he wanted comfort, you understand? The comfort of another person talking to him. He said nothing of importance. We talked of little things, like movies we enjoyed. But just before dawn he said something else.' Jacinto frowned with the effort of remembering. He tried to mimic Yellowthorn's Newcastle accent: '*You ain't a bad bloke for a wop. When you get out, give my old lady a message, and she'll see you right.*'

'A message? What was it?'

Jacinto looked pleadingly at Bergerac. 'It made no sense. But I tell you it all the same: *Well, sod off six hundred and thirty-one thousand, one hundred and fifteen.*'

'Oh, for God's sake!' Crozier said. 'What on earth – '

'That is what he said, sir. Please, I am telling the truth –

'Bernardo,' Bergerac interrupted. 'Was that all? Nothing more?'

'He gave me an address in London. When they let me go, I look for Mrs Yellowthorn. But she is not there.'

'She's dead,' Crozier said glumly. 'Took an overdose when she heard her husband had died. Of all the bloody luck.'

'Say the message again.' Bergerac scribbled it down at Jacinto's dictation. 'It would have meant something to Mrs Yellowthorn. And presumably to Quine and Marilyn. After all, they're willing to kill for it.'

Jacinto shivered. 'I think Marilyn would kill for very little. Maybe for nothing. It is amusing for her.'

Bergerac stared across the table. A thought had occurred to him. No one had told Jacinto that Marilyn had amused herself with Jorge Ferreira.

Without warning, Jacinto lunged across the table and seized Bergerac's hand. 'What will happen to me, sir? What will happen to that woman?'

Bergerac eased his hand away. 'I'm sorry, Bernardo. I just don't know.'

Oliver clattered down the companionway into the saloon. His nose was red with cold.

'Where's Ronny?' he asked. 'Not up yet?'

Norma Jean hesitated. 'He's in St Helier.'

'What?'

'He was unavoidably detained last night.' She spooned instant coffee and powdered milk into two mugs. 'He met an old friend.'

Oliver frowned. 'Look here, Marilyn – it's not good enough. I'm employing him, aren't I?'

'Don't worry. Here, pass me the kettle, will you?'

Oliver obeyed. He came within range of her perfume.

153

'It's a bit much, though,' he went on; his voice had lost some of its conviction. 'I mean, he's needed for the rota. And what happens if there's an emergency?'

Norma Jean edged closer. 'I thought you'd be pleased, Oliver.'

He licked his lips. 'What do you mean?'

She looked up at him and smiled. 'I must admit – I did encourage him to stay. I thought you'd be pleased. Two's company, eh?'

There was an answering smile on Oliver's face. He slipped an arm round her shoulders. She nestled closer. He nuzzled her hair with his mouth. Norma Jean stroked his chest lightly and then pushed him away.

'Later, Oliver,' she purred. 'First we must give the babies their breakfast.'

In the afternoon, the covered market was crowded with Christmas shoppers. Bergerac threaded his way through them. They were playing carols over the loudspeakers. Damn Christmas.

He plunged his hands into his pockets. He had left Jacinto at the Bureau – still weeping, beyond reach of consolation, for the wife and the cousin whom he felt he had destroyed. And they had died for a meaningless message: *Well, sod off six hundred and thirty-one thousand, one hundred and fifteen.* No, it had not been a good week.

Bergerac's fingers touched something hard and smooth. It was the key-ring without any keys – the .303 cartridge case which the kid had left at the Bureau. Matthew, that was his name. Another personal and professional failure.

In Halkett Place he paused, squared his shoulders and walked into the estate agency.

It would have been much easier to phone. Susan was in the back of the office, showing a video to a potential client.

'All the doors have electronic locks,' she was saying,

'including the patio doors. The swimming pool was rede-
signed last year. The vendors are particularly proud of the
water chute.'

She caught sight of Bergerac, excused herself to the client
and came towards him. He knew at once she was still
angry.

'Susan – '

'I'm afraid I'm busy,' she said firmly.

'Come to dinner. That's all I wanted to say.'

'Once bitten, twice shy.'

'But Susan – '

She turned and walked away.

'I'll be waiting for you,' Bergerac called after her.
'Outside the door, 5.30 sharp.'

'So sorry to have kept you,' Susan said to the client.
'Now that's the main drawing room. The ceiling moulding
is original but the fireplace is nineteenth century. The tiles
are lovely, aren't they? Seventeenth-century Dutch.'

'Susan!' Bergerac said loudly. 'I'm sorry, OK?'

Everyone in the estate agent's looked at him. Everyone
except Susan.

Bergerac tried to slam the door. It was spring-loaded, so
it swung shut behind him with the gentlest of hisses.

John Danston was almost happy.

The report was nearly finished. Only the conclusion
remained to be written. He rolled a new sheet of paper into
the typewriter.

This wasn't real: it was only a dream. In the dream the
Pilsen's tender was the hero. Heroes have to win, so
Danston was inventing reasons for it to succeed. He began
to type, using two fingers.

*The tenders have been scrutinized according to the following
criteria . . .*

When Emma came home they would have to celebrate –

155

perhaps go out for a meal. When Emma came home, everything would be all right. He would write another report and the new one would not be part of a dream.

Then the telephone began to ring.

As he walked away from the estate agent's, Bergerac passed the open door of a pub. The smell of beer beckoned him. Alcohol offered the surest road to oblivion: that was its main charm.

He shrugged the temptation away. He was off duty now until tomorrow morning. This afternoon was probably his last chance to find presents for Kim and Susan – not to mention for all the other people who had lesser claims on his purse and his imagination. He rebelled against the prospect.

The town oppressed him. He wanted to get away from crowds; they made him feel like a prisoner.

A prisoner like little Matthew pretended to be?

The memory of that small, freckled face was uncomfortable: it reminded him of yet another failure – a small one, admittedly, but they all counted. No, he decided: he couldn't face the Christmas shopping, not now. Maybe that rated as a failure too.

Instead, he collected the car and drove north out of St Helier. The weather was dry, but the sky held the promise of snow to come. The Triumph Roadster was not the best car for winter motoring: the hood had never fitted properly and the heater was temperamental. In his present mood, Bergerac was almost glad of the discomfort.

He crossed the island and parked on a headland that pointed at England. The northern coastline was rocky and dramatic; it suited his mood better than the soft undulations and sweeping beaches of the south. On his right, the grey expanse of St John's Bay stretched away to Fremont

Point. A rusty trawler was chugging eastwards, rolling in the swell. There were no other boats in sight.

Bergerac opened the glove compartment and took out a pair of field-glasses. Why shouldn't he go bird-watching if he wanted? Besides, he needed to stretch his legs.

The full force of the wind hit him as he got out of the car. In his pocket the car keys chinked against Matthew's key-ring. His stomach muscles, still sore from the events of last night, protested as he moved.

Huddled in a heavy coat, he walked along the rocky coastline. The only sounds were the cries of the gulls and endless grumble of the sea. St Helier belonged to another world. The tourists never saw this side of Jersey. Even the scenery was bleak and uncomfortable at this time of year. He decided he would go another hundred yards and then turn back. It was so cold that exercise had failed to warm him.

In any case, he was being bloody stupid. He had enough loose ends in his life without chasing after another. In all probability Matthew was back on the mainland by now. Coppers, Bergerac told himself glumly, shouldn't follow hunches, least of all in their spare time.

The path was harder to follow than it had been twenty or thirty years ago. Bergerac remembered coming here when old Vallier had the farm. The Valliers had held this land for generations. He wondered what the old man would have thought of an English millionaire living in his house.

A rocky outcrop forced the path to make a U-shaped detour. Beyond it, the path was blocked by a chain-mesh fence, topped with barbed wire. On the other side the path had been obliterated by a plantation of firs, probably planted as a windbreak.

Pilsen-Smith was perfectly entitled to enclose his land if he wanted. The path was not an official footpath. Still, the fence annoyed Bergerac more than he cared to admit.

Vallier would never have stopped people walking on his land, as long as they did no damage. There was suddenly no question of turning back.

He slung the field-glasses across his back out of harm's way and scrambled down the cliff. The last time he'd done this, he'd been bird's-nesting; and old Vallier had ticked him off and made him return the eggs. The farmer had softened the blow by giving young Jim a badge from a German forage cap. In those days Wehrmacht souvenirs had been plentiful on Jersey.

Bergerac reached the concrete post that marked the end of the fence, and swung himself round it. Soon he was in the shelter of the firs. The force of the wind abated abruptly; for a few seconds he felt warm.

The plantation was larger than it looked from the other side of the fence. The ground was spongy with dead pine needles. Not only was it warmer, it was much quieter – the evergreens absorbed and deadened the roar of the sea.

The trees ran parallel to the fence for about a hundred yards. Bergerac stopped. If he went much further, he would be in full view of the house. The authorities frowned on police officers who spent their leisure hours trespassing.

He worked his way back toward the sea along the side of the plantation furthest from the fence; he wanted to get an idea of the extent of the grounds. He reckoned that Pilsen-Smith must have about eight acres, excluding the farm's extensive garden. The land sloped sharply downwards. Bergerac remembered an inlet around here, guarded by a Martello tower built during the Napoleonic Wars. Vallier claimed his forebears used it for storing smuggled goods. It was unusual to find a Martello tower on this side of the island because of the strength of the natural defences.

The tower came into sight. At first sight it looked unchanged. It was a massive circular structure built of the local pinkish granite. The entrance was twenty feet above the ground on the landward side.

Bergerac took the field-glasses from their case and focused them on the tower. He began to notice the alterations that had been made in the last twenty years. The stonework had been repointed. Window frames had been replaced. A wooden staircase, scarcely more than a ladder, now led up to a heavy door which glistened with a new coat of black paint. The padlock on the door was obviously a recent addition.

At the bottom of the stairway he could see something on the grass. He blinked in surprise. Two steaming mugs were standing on a tray. They seemed completely out of place in this bleak, untenanted landscape. Who on earth would use the Martello tower for afternoon tea on a day like this?

The question barely had time to formulate itself in his mind. He heard a sharp expulsion of air, somewhere behind him. Something jabbed his leg: he cried out in pain.

Then the world went black.

CHAPTER
17

The daylight was draining away from the heavy clouds that covered the sky.

John Danston stood by the sitting-room window, struggling to make a decision. He had always hated to make up his mind. Decisions in a dream were even worse than in reality for there were no constant factors except fear and doubt.

A neighbour who was passing along the pavement with her children gave him a wave, but he failed to notice her. His eyes were focused on the glass itself: he was tracing sprawling capitals on the condensation, using the tip of his forefinger as the pen.

EMMA. PILSEN'S. COLTON. CHRISTMAS.

The outlines of the letters blurred even as he wrote them. They turned to water and trickled downwards. The window, he thought, was crying.

There were clouds in his mind as well as in the sky. On the arm of the chair beside him lay a buff-coloured folder. It contained his preliminary report on the Colton New Town tenders. He had typed it with two stumbling fingers on Emma's portable.

He knew he had done a good job. He had picked out the essentials of each tender and scrutinized them in detail. With the interests of the council and the rate-payers in mind, he had identified in each proposal the weaknesses, the strengths, the implications and – last but not least – those areas that the developer had preferred to leave vague.

Pilsen's, for example, had fudged the question of drainage in every section, largely ignoring the marshy nature of the site, in order to make their tender seem more attractive on grounds of cost. If adopted, their proposal would require years of expensive modifications.

They had used the same technique to deal with forecasts of traffic volumes on the new link road from Colton New Town to the city. Where possible they had based their calculations on the lowest figures in the estimated ranges; and they used them to justify a single carriageway road that ran dangerously close to the city's residential suburbs. But all the evidence suggested that even the upper figures of the estimates were too conservative. In Danston's opinion, the developer should take the link road by a longer route through open country; and he believed that the council should insist on the road being a dual carriageway for its full length.

With a sudden movement he smeared the blurred letters from the window. He had incorporated all these points in the main body of the report. Pilsen's seemed the most economical option at first sight; but that was only because they had cut so many corners – in the end, they might well be the most expensive. Moreover, the firm had a reputation for being a bit too sharp for its own good. A little-publicized but long-running case was going through the courts at present; the residents of a huge housing estate in the Midlands had banded together to sue Pilsen's for a series of constructional defects in their ten-year-old properties.

Yet Danston had backed the Pilsen's tender in his conclusion. It didn't matter, he told himself for the thousandth time, for it was only a dream. The voices on the telephone had ordered him to support Pilsen's, so he couldn't be held responsible. In any case, he had to do it for Emma's sake.

Nevertheless it was hard, even in a dream. The conclusion of the report went against all his professional experience; it pained him almost physically. If only Emma were here to advise him!

Advice – that was what he needed. The voices didn't want him to talk to people, but perhaps they would never know. Then perhaps he could make his dream decision.

He put his head in his hands. The stubble on his cheeks was rough to the touch. His eyes felt swollen; they chafed against their sockets. He could not remember when he had last eaten. It didn't matter. He didn't need food; he needed advice.

He glanced round the room as if he could find inspiration among the familiar furniture, the morass of papers on the floor and the unwashed mugs and glasses. Christmas cards lined the mantelpiece over the gas fire. His eyes rested on one of the larger ones: it was a reproduction of a winter scene by some nineteenth-century painter. Emma liked it – he remembered her talking about it. Skaters and stalls made a complicated pattern on the frozen surface of the Thames. In the background was the dome of St Paul's, massive against a leaden sky; and on the right was a bridge whose name he had forgotten; Emma would know.

The card was from Ned and Mary. *Ned*. Ned Arlen, the council's chief executive. Emma liked him – and so, for that matter, did Danston himself. Arlen would know what to do.

The telephone? He took a few paces towards it and then stopped. No – the phone belonged to the voices in his dream; they lived in the airwaves; it was more than likely they could listen in.

Better to go see Ned – it would be so much easier to

162

explain everything face to face. Ned was a good man – he understood. Last time he had been kind.

Last time? Danston's mind shied away from the memory. He sought relief in activity. Scooping the report into his briefcase, he ran into the kitchen and snatched the car keys from the rack over the door.

A stranger glared at him from the mirror by the sink. The face had staring, red-rimmed eyes, puffy skin and the beginnings of a beard. So they were watching him even in the house.

The discovery brought him close to the edge of panic. Maybe there was a watcher in every mirror. He burst through the door into the back of the garage. Routine, speeded up like the fast-forward on a video recorder, guided his actions: up with the garage door; unlock the car; throw the briefcase on to the passenger seat; clamber in; key in the ignition; try again when the engine failed to fire; try not to think what would happen if the bloody thing wouldn't start; try again –

The engine caught. Danston rammed the gear-stick into first and shot out of the garage. The car roared down the short, sloping drive, across the pavement and on to the avenue itself. Danston braked too late: he found himself on the wrong side of the road with his front bumper only inches from the opposite kerb.

A van hooted and skidded to a stop. The driver rolled down his window and swore. Danston muttered an inaudible apology, reversed and drove slowly down to the junction. He turned right towards the city.

An oncoming car flashed its lights at him. He realized that he had forgotten to switch on his own lights.

The incident had the curious effect of calming him. It was vital to take care. Nothing he did must attract the attention of the police; he was almost sure that they were in league with the voices in the airwaves. He could trust

Ned Arlen, but no one else – except Emma, of course; but she wasn't here.

Emma, darling –

His cheeks were wet with tears as he drove. He forced his mind to concentrate on all the important trivia of driving – traffic lights and speed limits, rights of way and lane discipline.

The journey was so familiar that the car almost steered itself. At the third roundabout he swung right on to the ring road. He took the second exit and then turned left at the next set of traffic lights. Then he was driving up the approach road to the council car park.

The offices loomed up before him. Two wings curved away from a huge central block. *Bad design,* Danston thought as he usually did when he parked here; *the orientation's wrong, the place is impossible to heat economically and it looks bloody awful too. Typical sixties' rubbish.* He edged the car into his reserved parking slot near the pretentious and absurdly draughty main entrance.

It was only when he had stopped the engine that he realized that the car park was nearly empty and that most of the windows were in darkness. He looked at his watch: it was after 6.30. In his dismay he beat his hands against the steering wheel. There was nothing for it but to drive to the Arlens' home, a converted farmhouse which was fifteen miles away.

But Ned sometimes worked late. Danston looked across at the chief executive's parking slot; Arlen's Volvo wasn't there. A Daimler was parked beside the empty space. The car was familiar. As Danston watched, the driver's door opened.

A portly figure struggled out and walked deliberately towards Danston's car.

Danston felt his mouth go dry. His hand twitched ineffectually and lay still; he was no more capable of turning the key in the ignition than a rabbit is capable of outstaring a stoat. *Of all the luck. Of all the bloody luck.*

Littledean tapped on the window. Danston rolled it down. The councillor's podgy hands rested on the sill. He bent down, bringing his face on to the same level as Danston's.

'John, you don't look well, really you don't. Why on earth have you come in?'

Danston made an inarticulate sound in the back of his throat.

Littledean's eyes fell on the briefcase.

'Don't say you've got Colton New Town on your mind? Maybe I can help. Want to talk about it?'

'I – I must go,' Danston said.

'You're in no state to go anywhere under your own steam,' Littledean said. 'You should be in bed. Emma shouldn't let you out of the house. Well, what's it to be? Shall I drive you home in my car or in yours?'

When Diamanté Lil reached the nightclub, she heaved a sigh of relief.

The big neon sign was alight, announcing to half St Helier that Lil's Place was open for business. Though it was still early in the evening, the foyer was crowded with a party of patrons who had just arrived. She guessed they were from the marketing conference at the Hotel de Bretagne. Despite the temporary absence of its proprietor, the nightclub was doing business as usual.

She paid off her taxi and walked slowly into the club. Her doctor had warned her not to overdo it. Jean-Luc caught sight of her and hurried across the room towards her.

'Madame! I was not expecting you until after the weekend. Are you sure this is wise?'

Lil grinned at him. 'It's better than moping at home. I

165

was going round the bend, just sitting there with the telly for company.'

'You must sit down,' Jean-Luc said. 'Let me take you upstairs to your office.'

She shook her head. 'I'm better off down here, with a few people around.'

'But the noise, Madame, and – '

'I'll sit quietly, I promise. I'll be a model customer, all right?'

Jean-Luc shrugged, recognizing defeat. He ushered Lil with great ceremony to a relatively secluded corner table; he insisted on protecting her privacy with a 'Reserved' sign. Jamie was dispatched for Perrier water and a smoked-salmon sandwich.

'Madame looks famished,' Jean-Luc said severely. 'You have not been looking after yourself.'

He hovered unobtrusively while she drank and ate. With a ruthlessness Lil had never noticed in him before, he screened the people who wanted to talk to her. Only the closest of friends were allowed to approach the holy of holies in the corner.

Among the privileged few were Deborah Hungerford and her daughter. Had it been Deborah alone Jean-Luc would have hesitated; but both he and Lil had a soft spot for Kim Bergerac.

'A night on the town?' Lil said as they sat down.

'We're meeting some friends,' Deborah said. 'Actually, we're fugitives.'

'What?'

'Dad wanted me to go to some stuffy dinner-party with him, at Guy Pilsen-Smith's. Do you know him? Looks a bit like a fish.'

'The builder? Yes, he's been in here once or twice.'

'How are you feeling?' Kim asked Lil.

'Almost normal, now I'm here. Jean-Luc's mothering me to death. It's lovely. All set for the disco?'

'Everything's organized, thanks to you and Susan,' Kim said. She glanced at her mother and added tactfully, 'And Mum and Grandad, of course. I just hope that people come – and that they enjoy it.'

'Don't you worry, they will,' Lil said.

There was a stir at the door and Lil automatically looked for the cause of it. Susan Young had just come in and was trying to negotiate her way through a tight knot of businessmen. Eventually the crowd parted. Lil noticed that Susan was still in her working clothes. Usually she changed for the evening. Jim Bergerac wasn't with her.

Once inside Susan looked round the club. Lil waved her over. Kim's face brightened as Susan approached. Deborah's smile displayed her perfectly capped teeth; if social dissimulation were an art form, the smile would have been a masterpiece.

Susan was obviously in a hurry, but her first questions had to do with Lil's health. While Lil was answering, Deborah's friends came in; she and Kim left the table.

When they were alone, Lil said, 'What's up with you? You look as if you need a stiff brandy.'

Susan shook her head. A lifetime in the licensed trade had made Lil an expert reader of faces. If she was any judge, Susan was miserable.

'Have you seen Jim?' Susan blurted out.

'Not since the morning after I got hit on the head. Is anything wrong?'

'I don't know where he is.'

'Well, if he's on duty – '

'No, you don't understand.' Susan fumbled in her bag for a handkerchief and blew her nose.

'Do you want to tell me about it?' Lil asked.

She felt an almost proprietorial interest in Jim Bergerac

and Susan Young. On their first date, Jim had brought Susan to the gala opening of Lil's Place. Ever since then Lil had watched the relationship develop with an anxiety which verged on the maternal. In her opinion, Susan was just the woman Jim needed; it was a pity, she felt, that Jim had so far failed to appreciate the full extent of his good fortune.

'We had a quarrel,' Susan sniffed. 'And it was all my fault.'

'I doubt it,' Lil said. 'Men can be so insensitive sometimes.'

The story came out in fits and starts. How Jim had been so wrapped up in the Ferreira case that he had forgotten their date last night; how he had even failed to be decently apologetic about it; how Susan had stormed out of his empty flat; and how she had spurned his attempts at reconciliation at the estate agent's this afternoon.

'But I didn't mean it, of course.'

Lil nodded wisely. 'Of course not.'

'He said he'd be waiting for me at 5.30 and I thought everything was going to be all right. But he wasn't there! I hung around for half an hour but he didn't turn up.'

'What did you do?'

'I was furious,' Susan snapped. 'What do you think? He's stood me up once too often. So I rang his flat and everywhere else I could think of. I even tried the Bureau. I was going to tell him it was all over. I've had enough of being used like a convenience, just when it suits him. But he wouldn't even give me that satisfaction. I could murder him. Have you ever known anything like it?'

'To be honest, yes.' Lil hesitated before deciding that now was not the moment for autobiographical confidences, however consoling they were meant to be. 'You thought Jim might be here?'

Susan shrugged. 'It was a possibility.' Her face hardened.

'It's the obvious place to bring a woman he wants to impress.'

'A woman? Come off it, love. I'd have his guts for garters.'

'Well, what other explanation is there? I reckon he's not so subtly giving me the elbow.'

Lil shook her head. 'No – not that. Not Jim's style at all. He's not devious, give him his due.'

'I wish I didn't care.' Susan's voice was desolate. 'He's a weakness of mine, that man – a fatal weakness, like drinking or something. Maybe I should found an organization for his former girlfriends.'

'Bergeracs' Anonymous?' Lil reached across the table and patted Susan's hand. 'Now stop being stupid. I know Jim and I know you. Remember the gala opening? That was the first time I saw you together, and I could tell how he felt about you even then. And it hasn't changed.'

'I wish I could believe you.' Susan bit her lip. 'But if he isn't with another woman, then where the hell is he?'

CHAPTER
18

The sea had somehow got inside his head. Bergerac could hear the waves flooding and ebbing, sucking greedily as they retreated.

A woman's voice said: 'I think he's coming round. Get some water.'

Bergerac liked the voice: it was calm and warm.

'It's that policeman,' a child said. 'I knew the police would come.'

Bergerac summoned up all his energy and forced his eyelids to open. Above his head was a roughcast stone vault. A naked electric bulb dangled from the ceiling; there was no other source of light. He could smell and hear the sea. Gulls were crying, somewhere far away. Old Vallier used to say that the gulls were the souls of drowned sailors, crying eternally for their lost loved ones.

A woman's face floated two feet above him. He frowned and tried to focus on it.

The policeman in him made an automatic inventory: brown eyes, a generous mouth, no make-up, tangled hair and the general appearance of someone who laughed a lot. The set of the jaw hinted at competence and determination. It was a nice face to have around – you could fall in love with the face's owner without much effort. The thought made him feel disloyal because of Susan. Susan? Something was wrong. He was meant to be meeting her at 5.30. That was a date he couldn't break. He tried to get up.

'Stay still.' The woman pushed him down. 'Just relax for a moment.'

Reassured, Bergerac closed his eyes again.

Sometime later he was drinking water, which was good because his mouth was dry; his teeth chattered against the enamel rim of the mug. The woman was supporting his head.

'Where the hell am I?'

'I was hoping you could tell us that.'

Bergerac pulled himself up so he could lean against the wall behind him. He realized that he was lying on a camp bed. The boy gave him a little nod of recognition. His freckled face was familiar. Bergerac groped through his memory for a name. Matthew? Matthew who? He gave up the effort and moved his limbs, one by one. All of them responded.

Both the woman and the child were wrapped in blankets. An elderly electric fire did little to take the chill from the air.

'Well?' the woman prompted him. 'Where are we?'

The question dispelled some of the haze in Bergerac's mind. The events of the last few hours began to return to him.

'Unless they moved me, we're in Saint John's Bay, near Old Highcliff Farm.' He glanced round the circular room. Wooden shutters masked deep embrasures in the walls. There was another camp bed and a bucket, but no other furniture. 'Probably in the Martello tower.'

'But where's that?'

He looked blankly at her for a moment. 'St John's Bay, you mean? On the north coast of the island.' He saw the question in her face and realized the extent of her ignorance. 'You're on Jersey, you know. The Channel Islands.'

'It's news to me,' the woman said drily. 'I'm Emma Danston, by the way. You've already met my son Matthew.'

'Detective Sergeant Jim Bergerac, Bureau des Etrangers. Would you mind telling me what's going on?'

Emma looked steadily at him. 'We were kidnapped a few days ago. Matthew and I were having a short holiday in Southampton, really to give my husband time to finish some work before Christmas. We were out walking when a man and a woman appeared. The woman had some sort of airgun, which she fired at me, then at Matthew. The next thing we knew, we were here.'

'They must have used the same thing on me. One of those animal tranquillizers?'

'Probably.' Her mouth tightened. 'Matthew's little finger got broken on the journey. When I found out, I made such a fuss they agreed to take him to the nearest Casualty Department, with me as a hostage for his good behaviour.' She ruffled her son's hair. 'But Matthew managed to give them the slip. Not for long, but time enough to find a police station. I . . . I thought that no one had believed him.'

Bergerac looked away. 'I'm afraid we didn't take it completely seriously. I'm here on my own. Any idea what this is all about?'

Emma shrugged. 'Only a guess. My husband's a planning officer. He's up to his eyes at present, assessing four tenders for a big job. You may have heard of it – Colton New Town?'

Bergerac nodded. His mind suddenly cleared. Scraps of information he had gathered over the last few days assembled themselves into a pattern.

'The Planning Committee will almost certainly go by his advice. My bet is that the kidnappers are putting pressure on John to recommend one of the tenders.'

'"Own Your Own Pilsen Home"?'

Emma looked sharply at him. 'Pilsen's are one of the firms.'

'This place is owned by a bloke called Guy Pilsen-Smith.

172

I gather he's the major shareholder. But wouldn't your husband call the police?'

'Not if they threatened to harm us.' Emma stared directly at him, as if challenging him to criticize her husband. 'John's a good man, but he's not a strong one. He had a nervous breakdown before we married. Well, it was worse than that, really. He got through it, but it wouldn't take much to push him back over the brink. We're more important to him than anything – a sort of sheet anchor to sanity. He'll be out of his mind with worry. He'll think it's a nightmare and he'll do whatever they tell him to do.' She lifted her chin. 'And I don't think the worse of him for that. I don't suppose you'll understand, Sergeant, but even the best people can have their weaknesses.'

'That's one thing I do understand.' Bergerac held her gaze for a moment. 'Help me up, will you?'

Bergerac, supported by Emma and Matthew, made a slow circuit of the room. He knew it was hopeless before they began. The walls were solid granite. The window shutters were held in place by padlocked steel bars. The door was seasoned oak. A fish-eye security lens had been inserted in the wood, five feet above the ground. It faced inwards, so whoever was outside could look into the room.

'It's no good,' Emma said wearily. 'We've tried all this a dozen times. When they bring us our meals, they make us stand up against the opposite wall, with our hands above our heads. Then they undo the two bolts. There's a lock too.'

'Who are "they"?'

'There are three of them altogether. The woman's a hefty blonde with dyed hair – she's the real boss, I think. One of the men is about my age – overweight, talks with a plum in his mouth. The other man's older – sounds like a Londoner. He's got a broken nose.'

'Do they all come?'

Emma shook her head. 'Only two of them at any one time – they take it in turns. One of them brings the tray and the other one carries a gun and does the door.'

'When's the next meal due?'

Emma looked at her watch. 'About half an hour. We usually get some sort of supper around eight o'clock.'

'It's 7.30?' Bergerac said. 'Are you sure about the time?'

'Yes. What's so important about it?'

Bergerac thought of Susan and wondered how she was feeling. He was two hours late already, and still counting.

'It doesn't matter,' he said. 'We've got to do something.'

Matthew said reproachfully: 'It's a pity you didn't bring your gun.'

'We don't carry guns here, you know.' Bergerac forced a smile. 'Sorry about that. We'll have to find another way.'

He tried to keep his voice light, but he had no illusions about the seriousness of the situation. Their captors had taken his wallet: by now they must know he was a copper. They couldn't afford to let their prisoners go. It was significant that they had allowed Emma and Matthew to see their faces: it implied that they had never intended to free them.

The woman was almost certainly Tuffnell's mysterious Marilyn, the specialist in contract kidnapping. Bergerac also had her to blame for the disaster last night. It looked as if she and Quine had been moonlighting – chasing Jacinto while they were meant to be guarding the Danstons.

As far as the kidnappers were concerned, there was an obvious solution to the problem of their three prisoners. There must be a boat in the inlet – how else could they have come over from the mainland with the Danstons? Three corpses, weighted with local granite, would disappear into the Channel.

'We've got to get out,' Emma said softly. Bergerac knew

from her face that she'd worked out the obvious solution too.

Matthew had moved away. He was sitting on a bed, as near as possible to the single bar of the electric fire. Bergerac stared down at his bowed head. The boy looked so completely vulnerable. He glanced at Emma and saw that she, too, was looking at her son.

It was always the kids who got hurt. He felt an immense anger for the sort of people who could so casually destroy a child out of greed – or indeed for any reason at all. The anger was so great that it blotted out both his fear and his physical discomfort. In that instant the idea came to him.

It was a ridiculous idea, the sort that could never work in real life. But it was the only one he had.

'Glad you could make it, Charlie. Come and get yourself warm.'

Pilsen-Smith clapped Hungerford on the shoulder and steered him towards the open front door. A woman with grey hair scraped away from her thin face was standing in the hall.

'I've put the drinks in the drawing room,' she said with a pronounced Scottish accent.

'Thank you, Mrs Jarrell. This way, Charlie.'

'I'm not too early, I hope,' Hungerford said; there were no other cars on the gravel sweep in front of the house.

'Not at all. In here.'

Hungerford coughed. 'In fact I hoped we might have a chance for a private word before the others arrived.'

The long, beamed drawing room was a discreet advertisement for its owner's wealth; Hungerford felt instantly at home.

'It'll be a pleasure,' Pilsen-Smith said. 'But first, how about a drink? You like a drop of Scotch, I remember. I've got a rather interesting sixteen-year-old Islay malt here. Care to try it?'

The whisky was superlatively good and tasted as if it were a hundred per cent proof.

'My son got it when he was up in Scotland,' Pilsen-Smith explained. 'Not bad, is it? It's a shame he can't be here tonight. We must have a foursome sometime, with him and your Deborah. Lovely lady.'

He raised his glass and drank to her.

'Ay,' Hungerford said, 'I'd like that. Look, Guy, I was wondering if you'd given any thought to that little matter I mentioned last time?'

'The Law and Order Committee?'

Hungerford nodded. 'There definitely will be a vacancy. I thought maybe we could have a little informal discussion after dinner. About ways and means, and so forth. If you're interested, that is.'

'Oh yes, Charlie. I'm very interested. It would be an honour.'

On the floor below them, the door to the outside world closed with a bang.

Two sets of footsteps ascended the stone stairs. Bergerac, Emma and Matthew had already lined themselves up along the wall opposite the door.

The footsteps stopped. Bergerac could almost feel the eye at the peephole boring into him. The first screech of unoiled metal took him by surprise. He tensed himself: *under starter's orders*. The second bolt was drawn back almost immediately afterwards. A key rattled in the lock.

Suddenly and simultaneously a blue flash ran round the room and a high scream cut through the air.

Emma dived to the floor and tugged the plug from the socket. The flex, which Bergerac had ripped away from the electric fire, now dangled harmlessly from the cast-iron handle on the inside of the door.

Bergerac turned the handle and burst into the little lobby on the other side of the door. There was a bulb here too, and it was still alight, because the lighting was on a different circuit from the power points. A blonde – Marilyn? – stared at him with her mouth open.

There was no time for finesse. Leaping over a tray which was on the floor, he cannoned into her with his shoulder and drove her back against the wall. It was a small revenge for what she had done to him last night.

The fat man had fallen back on the stairs. He lay head downwards, breathing stertorously through his mouth; as he fell, he must have caught the back of his skull on one of the treads.

Marilyn laughed.

Bergerac swung round and stopped abruptly.

He was staring at the muzzle of an automatic.

'Easy does it,' the blonde cooed. Her perfume eddied through the air. 'Just get back inside, like a good boy, or I'll – '

There was a blur of movement in the doorway to the room. The lights went out.

Instinctively, Bergerac dived for the woman's legs. She fired once: in that confined space it sounded like the crack of doom. Before he reached her, she screamed. He thudded into her. She was wriggling violently. Then she sucked in her breath and momentarily lost her grip on her attacker. Something warm and sticky dripped on to Bergerac's hand as he wrenched the gun away from her. *My blood or yours?* He flipped the woman on to her back and yanked her wrists up to her shoulder blades.

The lights came on. Marilyn swore viciously and lay still.

Emma Danston smiled down at Bergerac. She was standing by the light switches; in her hand was an empty

177

saucepan whose contents, some sort of stew, now dripped from the blonde's head.

Matthew ran to his mother and flung his arms around her waist. She stroked his head.

'It's all right, darling,' she said. 'We can go home to Daddy now.'

'Let's be honest about it,' Charlie Hungerford said. 'The States Police have got it easy. I mean, it's not like the mainland here.'

'Oh, quite,' the Attorney-General said. 'Guy, this hollandaise sauce is delicious.'

Hungerford persevered: 'And that's all the more reason why we're entitled to expect maximum efficiency from them. What happened last night just isn't on. It was a cock-up, if you'll excuse my French; there's no other word for it.'

'More wine, anyone?' Pilsen-Smith asked. 'What *did* happen last night, Charlie?'

'My ex-son-in-law bungled a surveillance operation.'

'Wasn't there an arrest?' the Attorney-General said.

Hungerford shrugged. 'If you can call it that. They're not even sure they've got enough evidence to hold him. No – it all proves my point: if we want the police to do a proper job, we need to give the Law and Order Committee a lot more teeth.'

Marilyn refused to talk. The man – Oliver David Pilsen-Smith, according to his driving licence – was in no condition to do so.

This was definitely the pair who had posed as Matthew's parents at the Bureau. When Bergerac searched Marilyn she spat at him. He found no evidence of identification – only his own wallet. There was an irony here: inside the wallet was a scrap of paper with Yellowthorn's cryptic

178

legacy written on it: *Well, sod off six hundred and thirty-one thousand, one hundred and fifteen.* She had what she wanted from Jacinto within her grasp. The fact that she left it in the wallet suggested that she had no more idea of its significance than Bergerac himself.

He locked the pair of them in the tower. Oliver Pilsen-Smith needed medical attention, but at present the Danstons' safety was Bergerac's priority.

He led Emma and Matthew towards the house; he didn't fancy the cliff path at this time of night. Guided by the lighted windows, they picked their way through the grounds to the farmhouse.

It was much colder out here in the open. The north-east wind had freshened since the afternoon. The roar of the sea was loud enough to make talking difficult. Bergerac gave Matthew his jersey and draped his jacket round Emma's shoulders.

The house itself was sheltered in a fold of land. It had changed beyond recognition since Bergerac had last been there. Powerful outside lights threw the repointed and repainted façade into relief. The tumbledown barns and stables had become garages and staff quarters. The morass of mud in the farmyard had been replaced with neatly raked gravel.

One of the garage doors stood open. Bergerac glimpsed two cars inside. A Jaguar XJS and a red Rover. Half a dozen cars were drawn up outside on the gravel. Bergerac pursed his lips in a silent whistle as he recognized Hungerford's Rolls.

He jerked his head toward the front door. 'Let's join the party.'

Emma caught his arm. 'Is that wise? Shouldn't we just get away?'

'It's the best thing to do. Unless you fancy a two-mile

walk. Besides, this sort of place has a lock on the main gate.'

The door was unlocked. The rumble of voices and the chink of cutlery guided them down the hall to the dining room. Bergerac opened the door without knocking. Emma and Matthew stood behind him in the doorway.

As they entered the eating and talking stopped abruptly. Bergerac was struck by the almost obscene contrast between the primitive conditions in the Martello tower and the warmth and luxury here. He was suddenly conscious of how the three of them must look – grubby, wild-eyed and desperate.

Most of the faces were familiar to him. He recognized the Attorney-General, a retired judge, a senator and two deputies – one of whom was Charlie Hungerford. The senator and the judge were both on the Law and Order Committee. The majority of the guests were accompanied by their wives. At the head of the table was a plump, sandy-haired man who bore a striking resemblance to a fish in a dinner jacket.

'Jim!' Hungerford scraped back his chair, breaking the spell that kept them all silent. 'What the hell – '

'Guy Pilsen-Smith? I'm Detective Sergeant Bergerac. You're under arrest.'

Bergerac was angry: he dominated the little gathering by force of personality. He explained in a few sentences exactly what had been going on.

Pilsen-Smith got to his feet. 'My dear Sergeant, I do assure you I knew nothing of this. Perhaps it's some madcap scheme of my son's – I really don't know. I've spent a lot of time on the mainland recently. I haven't been down to that tower for months.'

It was smoothly done. Pilsen-Smith effortlessly swept up the sympathy of his guests – powerful, wealthy men like himself, who hated scandal and protected their own kind.

Bergerac was suddenly convinced that the son and the blonde would back up the old man's story, that the wily old builder had foreseen this contingency and planned accordingly. No doubt Marilyn and Oliver would get the best defence lawyers available.

'You see, Jim,' Hungerford said, 'I knew there'd be a perfectly simple – '

'Excuse me,' Emma said politely. 'I'm afraid Mr Pilsen-Smith *is* involved. I recognize his voice. I heard him talking to his son and that woman when we arrived. They thought I was still drugged.'

Pilsen-Smith's mouth opened and closed. The tip of his tongue flicked along his lips.

Without warning he made a rush for the door.

A woman screamed.

Bergerac brought up Marilyn's pistol and rammed the barrel in Pilsen-Smith's stomach.

CHAPTER
19

The phone in the office rang shortly after midnight.

Jean-Luc answered it. Almost immediately he passed the handset to Lil, who had been persuaded to put her feet up on the sofa.

'Sergeant Bergerac, Madame.'

Lil leant across to the desk and switched on the speaker. 'Jim? What can I do for you?'

'Have you seen Susan? I've been trying to get hold of her.'

Lil glanced across the room. Susan, who was sitting in one of the armchairs, shook her head vigorously.

'Well, if she's here I can't see her.' Lil closed her eyes so the statement was no less than the literal truth. 'You've tried her home number, I suppose?'

'Of course I have,' Bergerac said. 'Sorry, Lil. I didn't mean to snap – it's been a rough evening.'

'Where are you?'

'At the Bureau. And the way things are shaping, I'll be here for another hour or two.'

'Trouble?'

'With a capital T. Still, it's more or less sorted out now. Look, can I leave a message for Susan in case she turns up? We had a date at 5.30, and I couldn't make it.'

'I hope you had a good reason.'

'At the time it seemed quite persuasive.' Bergerac's voice was dry. 'Someone gave me a dose of animal tranquillizer and put me behind bars. I didn't have much choice.'

Lil looked at Susan and raised her eyebrows. Susan shook her head again, though less vigorously than before.

'What's the message?' Lil said.

'Just say I'm looking for her and I'm sorry. She'll understand. I'll be at the flat after this, if she wants me. Damn it, Lil, you know what I mean.'

'Yes, Jim, dear,' Lil said. 'I think I do.'

The bells of St Helier were striking two in the morning by the time Bergerac got home.

He paused for a moment to listen to them. The wind had dropped and, though it was still cold, it was a beautiful night.

Professionally he had every reason to feel pleased, apart from the unsolved enigma of Yellowthorn's message. All the other pieces had dropped into place. They had even found the missing high-heeled shoe in Marilyn's suitcase. Emma had talked to John Danston on the phone; a doctor had seen him, and he was now staying with two friends, Ned and Mary Arlen.

Yet despite the success, Bergerac felt close to despair.

He looked up at his window. Suddenly his mood swung upwards when he saw the light shining through the crack between the curtains. He took the stairs three at a time.

Susan was curled up in a chair with a crossword puzzle on her knee.

She did not look up as he entered. Bergerac knelt by the chair and put his arms round her.

At first there wasn't much need for words. Some time later Susan stirred.

'Jim,' she said, 'what *did* keep you?'

It was a test question, he realized; though she had never said anything, he guessed that his automatic reticence about work was hurtful to her. In this case there was no reason why he shouldn't explain — none except his own reflexive attachment to professional secrecy.

Bergerac told her very nearly everything; he decided that it would not be wise to mention the precise nature of his reaction to Emma Danston. He even showed her the scrap of paper.

Susan read the words aloud: '*Well, sod off six hundred and thirty-one thousand, one hundred and fifteen.*' She repeated the words more slowly, rolling them round her mouth as though she were tasting them.

'The only people who knew what that meant were Yellowthorn and his old lady,' Bergerac said bitterly. 'Both of them are dead, so that's six million quid up the spout, barring a miracle.' He shrugged. 'Still, at least no one else is going to get killed for it.'

Susan was frowning at the piece of paper. Her face cleared.

'Rather childish, really,' she said.

'What? Have you seen something?'

She smiled at him. 'It's so obvious I'm sure everyone else has too.' The smile had a cutting edge to it. 'I know you detectives are trained to find solutions.'

'You know quite well that I haven't a clue what it means.' Bergerac was uneasily aware of the times he had mocked Susan's penchant for crossword puzzles and brain-teasers. 'Come on,' he pleaded. 'Tell me.'

'Not yet.' Susan rushed on before he could protest: 'You've got a road atlas for the mainland, haven't you? Can I have a look at it?'

'The Ordnance Survey one? Yes, here,' he said, going over to the bookcase.

He brought the atlas to her and watched as she turned the pages. Her face distracted him from the job in hand; she was astonishingly beautiful. At last she looked up and caught his eye.

'Well?' he demanded.

'I think I'm right,' she said calmly. 'What can you give me in exchange for a secret that's worth six million pounds in gold?'

Bergerac stood up and seized her hand.

'I can think of one thing,' he said, pulling her gently to her feet. 'I'd say it's priceless. Though whether you think it's worth six million quid is another matter.'

Susan allowed him to draw her towards the bedroom.

'We'll just have to see,' she said. 'I'll give you a free valuation afterwards, OK?'

The midday sun glinted on the planes on the runway. It was ten hours later, and Bergerac still hadn't done his Christmas shopping. He had been off duty this morning, but his time had been fully occupied. Susan believed in getting value for money.

The departure lounge was crowded with passengers waiting for their flight to London. Bergerac caught sight of a familiar face. He changed course away from the windows and headed for the bar.

Barney Crozier looked up. He was nursing a large gin and tonic, and for once he was smiling.

'I thought I'd come and say goodbye,' he said. 'They deserve the personal touch, don't you think?' He raised his glass and added unnecessarily: 'I'm celebrating.'

'Success?' Bergerac asked.

Crozier nodded. 'Gloucester CID phoned just before I left the Bureau. It *was* a map reference. SO 631115 – it's a disused well, slap in the middle of the Forest of Dean.'

'And they found the gold?'

'All there – down to the last ounce. It looks like Yellowthorn forced the security guard to help him unload before he shot him. What made you think of it?'

Bergerac temporized, caught between the desire to be

honest and the Chief Inspector's well-known disapproval of pillow-talk. 'It was something Susan said that gave me the idea.'

Crozier signalled to the barman. 'Have an orange juice or something,' he said expansively. 'Whatever you fancy. Four major arrests – not bad, Jim. And all of them are falling over to incriminate each other. That should keep the Committee off our backs.'

'For a day or two.' Bergerac turned to the barman. 'I won't have a drink, thanks.'

'Charlie Hungerford's pulling out his hair.' Crozier shook with silent laughter. 'You know he wanted Pilsen-Smith on the Committee?'

Bergerac shrugged. 'I'm not surprised. By the way, Barney, you're not going to press charges against Jacinto, are you?'

Crozier shook his head. 'I wouldn't dare. I had Lil on the phone this morning. She wants him back.'

There was another call for the British Airways flight to Heathrow. Bergerac looked anxiously towards the door. He turned back to Crozier.

'Have you heard from the Met?' he asked.

Crozier nodded. 'Overstone and Tuffnell have identified Marilyn. Her real name's Norma Jean Veldman. They even traced the bloke who sold her the tranquillizer gun. Now she's talking, they hope to tie up a lot of loose ends.'

'I still don't understand the Pilsen angle.' Bergerac glanced over Crozier's shoulder again: why were women always late? 'Pilsen-Smith was taking one hell of a risk.'

'He needed to. Pilsen's over-expanded last year. Three major creditors are planning to foreclose. The Colton contract meant the difference between surviving and going bust.'

Emma and Matthew came into the departure lounge, escorted by the WPC who had driven them from their hotel. Emma was wearing new clothes. Bergerac just hoped that John Danston deserved her.

'I nearly forgot your key-ring,' Bergerac said to Matthew while Emma was saying goodbye to Crozier. 'I meant to give it to you last night.'

He dropped it into Matthew's hand. The boy frowned. 'Why did you put the message back?'

Matthew pulled a roll of paper from the cartridge case and gave it to Bergerac. It was an old chocolate wrapper. The message was printed in straggling capitals: *HELP. FETCH POLICE. MY MUM AND ME ARE PRISONERS IN A TOWER BY THE SEA. MATTHEW DANSTON.*

'I did it in the toilet at the hospital,' Matthew said proudly. 'And left it in the police station. Clever, wasn't it?'

'Very clever.' Bergerac handed it back to Matthew. So much for his famous hunch. Emma was watching him with amused eyes; he suspected she realized what had happened.

The last call for the Heathrow flight came over the public-address system. Bergerac drew her aside.

'It was lucky you heard Pilsen-Smith,' he said. 'Saved the day. But why didn't you mention it before?'

Emma blushed becomingly. 'Well, I knew he was involved as soon as I saw him. Call it women's intuition. I couldn't let him get away with it, could I?'

'You mean . . .' Bergerac swallowed. 'You didn't hear him when they landed you at the inlet? You made it all up?'

'In a manner of speaking.' Emma grinned. 'I didn't wake up till after we reached the tower. But I knew Pilsen-Smith would have to meet the boat. The kidnapping was so important to him.'

'Well, I'm damned.'

'I'm sure you policemen never rely on intuition.' Emma held out her hand. 'But thank you for everything. You made the end of my stay a lot more enjoyable than the rest of it.'

'Emma – Mrs Danston,' Bergerac said. 'Jersey isn't always like this. Come in the summer. It's a great place for a holiday.'

He regretted the impulse as soon as the words were out. He had always had a weakness for attractive women. Come to think of it, this whole case had been about weaknesses – his own and other people's.

'The trouble is, Sergeant, holidays are just holidays.' Emma took Matthew's hand and smiled at Bergerac. 'You and I have to get back to real life.'

FOR THE BEST IN PAPERBACKS, LOOK FOR THE

In every corner of the world, on every subject under the sun, Penguin represents quality and variety – the very best in publishing today.

For complete information about books available from Penguin – including Pelicans, Puffins, Peregrines and Penguin Classics – and how to order them, write to us at the appropriate address below. Please note that for copyright reasons the selection of books varies from country to country.

In the United Kingdom: For a complete list of books available from Penguin in the U.K., please write to *Dept E.P., Penguin Books Ltd, Harmondsworth, Middlesex, UB7 0DA*

In the United States: For a complete list of books available from Penguin in the U.S., please write to *Dept BA, Penguin, 299 Murray Hill Parkway, East Rutherford, New Jersey 07073*

In Canada: For a complete list of books available from Penguin in Canada, please write to *Penguin Books Canada Ltd, 2801 John Street, Markham, Ontario L3R 1B4*

In Australia: For a complete list of books available from Penguin in Australia, please write to the *Marketing Department, Penguin Books Australia Ltd, P.O. Box 257, Ringwood, Victoria 3134*

In New Zealand: For a complete list of books available from Penguin in New Zealand, please write to the *Marketing Department, Penguin Books (NZ) Ltd, Private Bag, Takapuna, Auckland 9*

In India: For a complete list of books available from Penguin, please write to *Penguin Overseas Ltd, 706 Eros Apartments, 56 Nehru Place, New Delhi, 110019*

In Holland: For a complete list of books available from Penguin in Holland, please write to *Penguin Books Nederland B.V., Postbus 195, NL–1380AD Weesp, Netherlands*

In Germany: For a complete list of books available from Penguin, please write to *Penguin Books Ltd, Friedrichstrasse 10 – 12, D–6000 Frankfurt Main 1, Federal Republic of Germany*

In Spain: For a complete list of books available from Penguin in Spain, please write to *Longman Penguin España, Calle San Nicolas 15, E–28013 Madrid, Spain*

FOR THE BEST IN PAPERBACKS, LOOK FOR THE

PENGUIN BESTSELLERS

Is That It?   Bob Geldof with Paul Vallely

The autobiography of one of today's most controversial figures. 'He has become a folk hero whom politicians cannot afford to ignore. And he has shown that simple moral outrage can be a force for good' – *Daily Telegraph*. 'It's terrific . . . everyone over thirteen should read it' – *Standard*

Niccolò Rising   Dorothy Dunnett

The first of a new series of historical novels by the author of the world-famous *Lymond* series. Adventure, high romance and the dangerous glitter of fifteenth-century Europe abound in this magnificent story of the House of Charetty and the disarming, mysterious genius who exploits all its members.

The World, the Flesh and the Devil   Reay Tannahill

'A bewitching blend of history and passion. A MUST' – *Daily Mail*. A superb novel in a great tradition. 'Excellent' – *The Times*

Perfume: The Story of a Murderer   Patrick Süskind

It was after his first murder that Grenouille knew he was a genius. He was to become the greatest perfumer of all time, for he possessed the power to distil the very essence of love itself. 'Witty, stylish and ferociously absorbing . . . menace conveyed with all the power of the writer's elegant unease' – *Observer*

The Old Devils   Kingsley Amis

Winner of the 1986 Booker Prize
'Vintage Kingsley Amis, 50 per cent pure alcohol with splashes of sad savagery' – *The Times*. The highly comic novel about Alun Weaver and his wife's return to their Celtic roots. 'Crackling with marvellous Taff comedy . . . this is probably Mr Amis's best book since *Lucky Jim*' – *Guardian*

Castaway Lucy Irvine

'A savagely self-searching tale . . . she is a born writer as well as a ruthlessly talented survivor' – *Observer*. 'Fascinating' – *Daily Mail*. 'Remarkable . . . such dreams as stuff is made of' – *Financial Times*

Runaway Lucy Irvine

Not a sequel, but the story of Lucy Irvine's life *before* she became a castaway. Witty, courageous and sensational, it is a story you won't forget. 'A searing account . . . raw and unflinching honesty' – *Daily Express*. 'A genuine and courageous work of autobiography' – *Today*

The Adventures of Goodnight and Loving Leslie Thomas

Sometimes touching, sometimes hilarious, sometimes alarming, the adventures of George Goodnight represent a quest for excitement and love. 'A constant pleasure. Leslie Thomas is to the contemporary novel what Alan Ayckborn is to the Theatre: a wry humorist with the rare ability to make his audience feel as well as laugh' – *Sunday Telegraph*

Wideacre Philippa Gregory

Beatrice Lacey is one of the most passionate and compelling heroines ever created. There burns in Beatrice one overwhelming obsession – to possess Wideacre, her family's ancestral home, and to achieve her aim she will risk everything; reputation, incest, even murder.

A Dark and Distant Shore Reay Tannahill

'An absorbing saga spanning a century of love affairs, hatred and high-points of Victorian history' – *Daily Express*. 'Enthralling . . . a marvellous blend of *Gone with the Wind* and *The Thorn Birds*. You will enjoy every page' – *Daily Mirror*